Ethan shoved his hands into the front pockets of his jeans. "You date real cowboys?"

"Not so far." Bella looked at him quizzically. "Funny. I never thought of you as a cowboy."

"How did you think of me?"

"It wasn't easy. I had to deal with a certain mental block. But look at you now. You've got the boots, the Wrangler jeans, the hat." She smiled. "That hat looks as though it could tell some campfire stories."

He tapped her arm with his hat. "You're keeping me in suspense here, woman. My ego ain't what it used to be. But I'll tell you what. After the rodeo, I'll take you dancing."

"Oh, that's a real incentive. You know how long I've avoided dancing?" He cocked an eyebrow, and she nodded. "Yes. That long."

"The wait is finally over, baby. Wolf Track is back."

Dear Reader,

Throughout the time I've been working on my "Double D Wild Horse Sanctuary" series of books, I've been looking forward to creating Ethan Wolf Track's story. I love a good bad boy, and that's exactly who Ethan is. He's been in touch with his brother, rodeo cowboy Trace Wolf Track, and he ran into his father, Logan, at the Double D. But his relationship with Logan has been strained in recent years. Sent to prison for a crime he didn't commit, this hometown hero has become a man apart from family and friends.

But at least one of his old friends hasn't forgotten him. Bella Primeaux was a smart, shy high school underclassman when she last saw Ethan, and she's the first to admit she had a secret crush on him. But carrying a torch was never her style. Now that Ethan's a free man and Bella an independent professional woman—a local celebrity as a TV news reporter—what could they possibly have in common?

South Dakota is one of my favorite settings. It's where I met my husband. It's a place where the sky is so big and powerful it takes your breath away. It's a land so vast, so nearly natural, that freedom would seem to reign. But freedom can sometimes be an elusive dream, and without love the dream can feel hollow. A good bad boy is bound to keep his feelings to himself.

Until the right woman comes along.

Please visit me on Facebook and on Riding With The Top Down, my blog on Wordpress. Enjoy the ride!

All my best wishes,

Kathleen Eagle

THE PRODIGAL COWBOY

KATHLEEN EAGLE

HARLEQUIN®
entertain, enrich, inspire™

Recycling programs
for this product may
not exist in your area.

ISBN-13: 978-0-373-65691-2

THE PRODIGAL COWBOY

www.Harlequin.com

Printed in U.S.A.

KATHLEEN EAGLE

published her first book, a Romance Writers of America Golden Heart Award winner, with Silhouette Books in 1984. Since then, she has published more than forty books, including historical and contemporary, series and single title, earning her nearly every award in the industry. Her books have consistently appeared on regional and national bestseller lists, including the *USA TODAY* list and the *New York Times* extended bestseller list.

Kathleen lives in Minnesota with her husband, who is Lakota Sioux. They have three grown children and three lively grandchildren.

For All My Relatives

Chapter One

"Looks like he ain't coming."

Bella Primeaux glanced up from the news report on her smartphone display. The cowboy claiming the next bar stool was half-shot and full-ugly. She didn't know him, wasn't interested in knowing him, and there was no point in sparing him more than a glance. She pressed her elbows against the bar and swiveled two inches to the right, turning a cold left shoulder.

"What's that you're drinkin'?"

Bella glanced right. Another one was moving in. She was book-ended by Crude and Rude. Experience told her that if they got no satisfaction, their type would go away.

"What does that look like to you, Loop?" the one on the right asked the one on the left. "Seven and seven?"

Loop? Bella swallowed the urge to laugh. She'd interviewed a rodeo cowboy named Rope who'd given a shout out to his brother Cash and his friend Spur. But *Loop?*

"Looks like tea." Loop was perceptive.

"Is that some of that Long Island iced tea? You wanna try some, Loop?" Rude signaled the bartender. "Bring us three more of these."

"Lemme try hers first," Loop said as he reached for Bella's glass from the left.

She slipped her phone into the woolen sack that hung over her shoulder on a braided cord. He could have her drink. She was leaving anyway.

"Is it whiskey and tea?" Loop sniffed, slurped and slammed the glass on the bar. "It's just tea."

"And it's yours now, Loopy," said a newcomer to the growing group.

Bella turned to her left, and her glance traveled quickly over the glass in the one called Loopy's grubby hand, past the full-ugly face to a faintly familiar one that loomed in the shadows above Loopy's cowboy hat. Familiar, fine looking, and frankly unsettling. It had been years since she'd seen the man, but he wore the years as well as his own straw cowboy hat. Surprising, considering where he'd spent the last couple of those years. His hat was battered, and his jeans and T-shirt had seen better days, but he made them look camera ready. She'd lost what little touch she'd had with high school friends, and Ethan Wolf Track was no exception, but she'd never quite shaken her interest in what he was up to. Generally it was no good.

But his smile was as disarming as ever.

"Sorry I'm late, Bella."

Loopy peeked over his shoulder and then turned back to Bella with a whole new brand of interest in his glazed eyes. "Why didn't you just say you were with Ethan Wolf Track? Hell, man, we were just—"

"Long Island iced tea all around. Loopy's buying." Ethan's hand appeared on Loopy's shoulder. "Right, man?"

"It's just tea. There's no whiskey," Loop said.

"Long Island iced tea isn't made with whiskey or tea." Ethan jiggled his hand rest. "You been living under a rock, Loopy?"

"Same as you."

"Nah, look at the difference." Ethan laid his hand on the bar beside Loopy's. "You need to get yourself some sun, boy."

Bella glanced between the two faces. The "boy" couldn't have been any younger than the man, but he didn't take exception. Ethan was still *the man*. The memory of a younger but no less commanding Ethan letting the boys know who was boss flashed through her mind.

"Iced tea for two," the bartender announced, landing the glasses on the bar with a thunk. "As for the other two, you want another beer? It's the same price as tea."

"No beer for these horses, Willie," Ethan said as he claimed both glasses. "Tricky, ain't it, Loopy? Pullin' the wagon and riding it, too?"

"You got your parole officer, I got mine. Far as I'm concerned, beer don't count," Loopy grumbled. "And it's *Toby*. That's a Toby Keith song, 'Beer For My Horses.'"

"Not without Willie," Ethan said as he glanced at Bella and gave a nod toward a corner booth. "Not on my wagon."

Bella was off the bar stool, but she wasn't looking for a booth, and the man and his boys could do what they pleased with their wagon. She wouldn't be vying for a parking spot at the Hitching Post. She'd already crossed the place off her list of possible sites for her report on Rapid City's hottest singles' hangouts.

"Would you rather go someplace else?" Ethan asked her quietly.

She looked up, taken by the change in his tone. He was speaking for her benefit alone, and he sounded sincere, even hopeful. Tension drained from her shoulders as she shook her head. "We can catch up right here."

As she neared the high-backed booth, she saw a big book lying open on the far side of the table beside a cup half-filled with black coffee. She slid into the near side, her back to the room.

"Looks like he ain't comin'," she drawled as she checked her watch.

"Maybe he's still working on his story." He set his glass on the table and dropped his hand over the book, which he closed, swept off the table and deposited on the seat beside him in one quick motion. His eyes danced. "Better be a good one, huh?"

She shrugged, subtly acknowledging that he was playing along. "You were here all along. All I saw was the hat."

"It serves many purposes." He pulled down on the brim, shadowing all but the generous lips and their slight smile.

"I'm surprised you remember me."

"I watch TV."

"So…you don't actually *remember* me."

"Really took me back when I saw you sitting on that bar stool. You sat in front of me in—what class was it? English?"

"History."

"History. Don't remember any names or dates, but I never forget a woman's back. You have a small—" he hooked his hand over his shoulder and touched a spot near the base of his neck "—beauty mark right here."

"*Beauty* mark?" She laughed. "It's called a mole."

"Not in my book."

"Which book is that?" She wondered about the one he was sharing his seat with.

"History. My favorite class. Liked it so much, I took it twice." He dropped his hand to the seat as he leaned back, grinning. She imagined him patting that book as though he wanted to keep a pet quiet. "You were there the second time around."

"No wonder you had all the answers. You'd already heard the questions."

"I didn't hear anything the first time." He leaned closer, getting into the reminiscence. "We did a project together. Remember?"

"I wasn't going to mention it. You still owe me."

"I do?"

"I bought all the materials. Actually, I did all the work. You were going to come to my house the night before it was due, but you never showed up."

"Forgot about that part." He arched an eyebrow and cast a pointed glance at her watch. "How do you keep getting mixed up with guys like that?"

"I'm not meeting anyone," she confessed.

"Then what the hell are you doing here?" He pulled a dramatic grimace as he glanced past her.

She shrugged. "Checking the place out."

"For what? This ain't no singles' bar, woman. This is a hole in the wall."

"Maybe I'm not single. Maybe I'm here doing my job." She gave herself a second to rein in her rising tone. "And maybe I didn't need to be rescued."

"In the old days, you wouldn't've said *maybe*. Once you got to talkin', you were as sure and self-determined as any girl I ever met." He gave her the no-bull eye. "I don't know about the rest, but you're not married."

"That doesn't mean I'm single."

"I think it does." He took a drink of his tea, then looked at her again. "So how much do I owe you for labor and materials?"

"Since it was a required class, I think you owe me your diploma."

"I showed up for the report. I had all the facts and figures. Hell, we got an A, didn't we? Can't do any better than that." He shook his head. "We'll have to come up with something else. You sure don't need my diploma."

"And you sure have a better memory than you first let on." She gave a tight smile. "I guess we can call it even. Being Ethan Wolf Track's history project partner raised my lowly underclass social status a notch."

"What were you, a sophomore?"

She shook her head.

"Freshman?"

She smiled and nodded.

"How did you get into that class as a freshman, for God's sake?"

"I took a test. Actually, I took several. They had a hard time coming up with a schedule for me." She lifted one shoulder. He had his muscles, she had her brain. "And you were a senior and the captain of everything."

"You were smart. It didn't take a test to figure that out. You were goin' places." He glanced around the room. "Better places than this."

"I go where the story is. Or where we think it might be." She tested out a coy look as she sipped her tea. "Stay tuned."

"Do me a favor. Give me a heads-up if this place is gonna be raided. I try to stay out of trouble these days."

"By doing what?"

"I guess you could say I'm a cowboy."

"Like your brother?"

"Not a rodeo cowboy like Trace. A working cowboy. A ranch hand. I work for the Square One Ranch."

She had no idea where that was, but he seemed to think the name of the place spoke for itself, so she made her usual mental note. *Find out. It could lead to something.*

"So you're one of a dying breed," she said. "I did a story on a guy who calls himself a cowboy for hire. He says he has more work than he can handle. Do you ride a horse or an ATV?"

"What's an ATV?"

"All terrain…" She caught the smile in his eyes. "You know, vehicle."

"Those kid toys? Couldn't call myself a cowboy

if I rode one of those things. Hell, I was raised by Logan Wolf Track."

"He trains horses, doesn't he?"

"He does, and so do I. I'm training a mustang right now. Entered up in a contest." He winked at her. "Gonna win it, too."

Déjà vu on the Wolf Track wink. She'd been on the receiving end of one or two of those babies years back, and the experience had given her the same tummy tickle that was *not* going to get a smile out of her now.

"You're talking about the competition they're running at the new Wild Horse Sanctuary near Sinte?"

"The wild horse program is pretty new, but the Double D Ranch has been there forever," he reminded her. "I hired on for a couple of summers when I was a kid, back when old man Drexler was running it. Now it's his daughters."

"I know. I've been reading up on the place." She took a breath, a moment's pause. They'd been playing a circuitous game, and she'd just landed at the foot of a ladder. One person's connections could be another person's rungs. They could be fragile, but as a journalist, she was weightless. Most sources had no idea she'd gotten anything from them.

But Ethan Wolf Track wasn't most sources. Sure, he'd been a source of adolescent anxiety and disappointment, but hadn't that been his job back then? It was up to the captain of everything to teach the princess of nothing not to expect too much. Bella had always been a quick study.

Still, he owed her.

"I think it's wonderful, the way the Drexlers have worked out a deal with the Tribe to set aside some of that remote reservation land for more sanctuary."

The Tribe being her people and Ethan's adoptive father's people. Logan Wolf Track was a Lakota Sioux Tribal councilman. Ethan looked Indian, too, but she'd never asked him about his background. Everyone knew that his mother had left Logan to raise her two boys, whom he'd legally adopted—just up and left and never came back—but nobody asked too many questions. It wasn't their way. Ethan and his older brother, Trace, were Wolf Tracks.

"Are you working on a news story?" he asked.

"I've been digging around." She folded her hands around her glass and studied the two shrinking chunks of ice. "There's definitely a story there— one that goes back a ways—but I'm looking for the details on my own. It's not the kind of assignment I'm likely to get from KOZY-TV."

"Why not? They don't like mustangs?"

"They're fine with mustangs. They don't like digging around."

"Isn't that how you come up with news? Dirt sells."

"But sleeping dogs don't bite, and the suits at the station—such as they are here in good ol' Rapid City,

South Dakota, you know, not exactly coat and tie—they don't want to get their business-casual clothes torn." She ignored his quizzical look. "Let's just say they don't pay me to dig." She smiled. "But it's fun, isn't it? You dig?"

He chuckled. "Postholes, yeah."

"When you were hiring out as a kid, did you ever work for Dan Tutan?" The change in his eyes—quizzical to cold—was barely discernible, but it was there. "You know, the Drexlers' neighbor."

Oh, yeah. He knew.

But he shook his head. *Interesting.*

"There's a story there," she said with a smile. "Big-time rivalry. Maybe some political back-scratching going on that could affect Indian Country. And that's where I come in. Like I said, strictly on my own." Was he ready for the kicker? Timing the kicker was Bella's journalistic specialty. "Tutan wants the leases that went to the Double D for the sanctuary, and he's got a friend in D.C.—Senator Perry Garth."

He stared at her. Or *through* her.

Perfect timing.

"South Dakota's beloved Senator Garth. Tutan and Garth go way back. And Garth is on the Indian Affairs Committee, as well as the Subcommittee on Public Lands and Forests."

"Politics." He shook his head. "You just cruised past my point of interest. My story's in the training competition. My interest is in the horses." He drank half of what was left in his glass in one deep pull.

"I just thought…because Logan is on the Tribal Council…"

"That's *his* story." He set the glass down and smiled as he slid to the end of the booth. "You wanna talk politics, you're followin' the wrong Wolf Track." He glanced toward the bar and its deserted stools. Remote control in hand, the bearded bartender was surfing channels on the screen above the Bud Light sign. "Looks like your fans have moved on."

"I doubt that pair watches much news. They know *you,* though."

"Yeah. You need a name to drop in low places, you're welcome to use mine." He gave her his signature wink again. Damn if it didn't give her the same deep-down shiver. "You decide to do a story on wild horses, look me up."

And *damn* if he didn't walk out first, taking the book she hadn't been able to identify.

Ethan sat behind the steering wheel of his pickup, parked in the shadows across the street from what had once been the Hitching Post. The neon had given up the ghost on the letter *H,* so it was now the *itching Post.* The sign had called out to him the first time he'd seen it. He'd finally had his freedom back— most of it, anyway—and it had some weight to it. He was itching to do something different with his life, but damned if he knew what. So he'd answered the blinking call of the itching Post. He'd claimed a bar stool, wet his whistle after a long dry spell and gotten himself wasted. *Stupid* drunk.

The next morning he'd looked at himself in the mirror and scratched his face. He'd scratched his neck, his shoulder, dug all his fingers into his hair, looked in the mirror again and nearly busted a gut laughing.

The sign said itching post, you idiot. Not scratching post.

If he'd learned one thing from spending two years behind bars, it was that the word *freedom* pretty much summed up everything a man had to lose. Freedom was living. Two years without it and you had a foot in the grave. Deadwood. Reviving that foot meant getting a leg up somehow. He hadn't been quite ready for South Dakota. He still had some growing up to do.

He'd gone to Colorado—as good a place as any that wasn't South Dakota—and taken up his parole officer's suggestion that he continue on the path he'd taken with the Wild Horse Inmate Program. Ethan had answered correctly—*yeah, I like that idea*—but mentally he'd added that the prison program couldn't claim credit for anything except maybe backing him into the right corner, the one that gave him a clear view of where he'd come from and where he might go. He'd spent most of his life within earshot of a horse barn, which might have been why he'd taken horses for granted, along with every other promising path he could have taken instead of the one that had cut off his slack.

Before the horses—before Logan Wolf Track—his life was hazy. He'd been Trace's little brother. They'd had a mother, but she was part of the haze. Even after she'd married Logan, her part of the family equation was hazy. *Muddy,* more like. He remembered the sound of her voice and the way she'd drawn out certain words so that South Dakotans looked at each other and shrugged. An accent, they'd called it, but to him it was the sound that settled an unsettled mind. *Mom's here.* He couldn't picture her face, but he still felt an odd sense of relief when he heard her voice, even though it was only in his head. He was up to his neck in hot water, hot *muddy* water, shrouded in early-morning haze, but he wasn't alone. He could hear her. She hadn't gone away.

And neither had that stupid kid. God, how he hated that quivering, shivering little boy who still clung to the soft tissue of his innards. He was pitiful, that kid. He had to get tough or get dead, that kid, and he'd damn sure better not show his face. Keeping that kid quiet had been a full-time job. Ethan needed all the help he could get, and he'd assigned roles. Whether they knew it or not, every person, place or thing within spitting distance had a part to play, and he'd taken it all for granted.

Including the friendship he might have had with the woman who'd just stepped into the spotlight under the itching Post sign. Of course he remembered her. Straight-A student with a straight body and a straightforward approach. She would go places and do things, and she wasn't letting anyone get in her way. Not that his charm was lost on her, or that he wouldn't pass up the chance to use that to his advantage, but there was an air of dignity about her that gave her some protection from guys like him.

But not from guys who had no use for dignity.

Tom "Loopy" Lupien and his forgettable sidekick were back in play, following Bella out the door. Two colorless figures casting long shadows across the dimly lit sidewalk. He'd thought they were gone. Must have been hiding out in the can.

"Hey, did the Wolf make tracks?" one of them called after her.

"You need a ride?" the other asked. In this light it was hard to tell one from the other, but it didn't matter. Any friend of Loopy's had been scraped from the mold underneath the empty barrel.

A remote-control lock chirped, headlights flashed, car door opened and shut, engine roared. Bella was safe. Ethan smiled to himself. No-nonsense Bella.

No sooner had she turned onto the street when another engine fired up. An old Ford pickup—even older than Ethan's rattletrap Chevy—emerged from the lot behind the building and followed her car.

Damn. Loopy wouldn't be able to bring any prey down himself. He was a scavenger. The other one must've been driving. Between the two of them, they could do some damage.

Ethan joined the parade. When they reached a one-way residential street, Bella parked her little white Honda on the curb near the front entrance to a modest two-story apartment building. Ethan peeled away from Loopy's tailgate, pulled over to the opposite curb, and watched Loopy and his pal roll past Bella's parked car. They'd taken the hint. Ethan chuckled. *My job here is done.*

Bella hopped out of her car, slammed the door and turned toward Ethan's pickup, gripping some kind of bag made out of blanket material with a string handle—was it a purse, or a grocery sack?—under her arm.

"Hey! I carry a .38 Smith & Wesson, and I know how to use it!" she shouted across the street. "So whatever you're thinking, think again."

Her face was hidden in the shadows, but her hands were steady, her shoulders squared and her long black hair shone blue-white under the streetlight. He didn't know who she thought she was talking to, but she wasn't bluffing.

And he loved it.

He was thinking, *I've got your back.* Not that she needed him, but he was there, just in case.

Hell of a woman, he told himself as he watched

her stand her ground. She was on TV, but that was just a job. It wasn't her life. Pretty cool. Cool enough to get the message without some big explanation to go with it. Whatever her interest was in Senator Perry Garth—the man who'd helped put Ethan away for two years—it was of no interest to *him*. Neither was any rivalry between neighbors, nor tribal politics. Ethan was looking for a new life. He wanted the kind of freedom Bella had—the opportunity to chart her own course, to do a job and then some, and that some could be more than what somebody else was willing to pay for.

The last time he'd seen her, she'd been a sweet young girl with a big brain. He'd assigned her brain a role, but the girl was sweet and young, and she'd had that straight body and those big ideas. Sure, she'd had the hots for him, but back then she'd been more appealing walking away from him in a huff than looking up at him all wide-eyed and innocent. She'd had some growing up to do.

She turned and mounted the steps to the front door.

I've still got your back, Bella, but I can appreciate your front now, too. Turn around. Let me see those pretty eyes.

No such luck. She pushed the door open and disappeared.

Ethan grinned as he shifted out of neutral. Yes, sir, little Bella Primeaux had grown up just fine.

Chapter Two

The tiny reservation town of Sinte, South Dakota, hadn't changed much, but the house Bella had grown up in looked different. In only five years weeds had taken over Ladonna Primeaux's flower beds. A swing set occupied what had been the vegetable garden, and an old Jeep had muscled in on the shrub roses that still more or less lined the driveway. Mom had fussed over that yard the way some women gravitated toward babies. With her gone, it looked like most of the other yards in the neighborhood—a cottonwood tree or two, a bunch of kids' toys, maybe a deck and some struggling grass.

Bella could hear her mother now. *Don't ever let your yard go, Bella. All it takes is a little interest.*

People who take an interest, those are the interesting people. They're the ones you always want to talk to.

Ladonna Primeaux was an interesting person. Everyone thought so. Bella had been certain of it. Her mother was as knowledgeable as she was opinionated, which was fine by Bella. Nothing wrong with having opinions if you had the knowledge to back them up. Mom was also dependable, practical and psychic. It wasn't always easy being the only child of a woman who was constantly one step ahead of the one Bella was about to take. But she'd followed the deep imprints of her mother's footsteps until there were no more.

The home they'd shared wasn't there anymore, and the house alone gave no comfort. No point in lingering, hoping for more than memories. Bella didn't need guidance or approval anymore—she knew who she was and where she was going—but with her mother's death she'd been cut off at the roots. She was growing as a journalist, but every time she looked at her résumé, she felt like a fraud. Maybe not on the outside—she had the look, totally—but deep down she was missing something.

Her KOZY-TV News assignments rarely touched on Indian issues, so she'd started blogging as Warrior Woman, and her site was gaining followers. But the comments from people who claimed to be Native were few and far between. Maybe they were out there but just weren't saying so. Or maybe they weren't even there. Maybe what was missing was new growth. Her interest in Lakota issues was real, but what about Lakota life? What about the home she'd left as quickly as she could and the mother who'd encouraged her daughter to fly while she'd remained in the nest? What about the remnants of those severed roots? Deep down they were still there, like shorn whiskers creating an itch that needed attention.

Guess what, Bella, you're not a kid anymore. You need to touch up your roots or grow some new ones.

A stop sign and two right-hand turns took her to Agency Avenue. The old Bureau of Indian Affairs building with its spacious offices had been turned over to the Tribal government, and the BIA had moved into the building once occupied by the Tribe. Sign of the times, Bella thought as she took in all the changes. There were more windows, fewer walls, and the colors of the four directions—red, white, black and yellow—had replaced BIA green and tan. There were new names on the directory. Indian names. But there were no office numbers, and so she asked the receptionist whether Councilman Logan Wolf Track was in the house. *He's around here somewhere* was the old familiar answer. Monday-through-Friday casual.

"Of course I remember you." Logan greeted her with a handshake when he came out to greet her. He was lankier than his son but not as tall, not quite as handsome. "Full scholarship to a fine college on the East Coast, right?"

"University of California at Berkley."

"I meant West Coast." He smiled easily. "I remembered the important stuff. Full scholarship, terrific college and Bella Primeaux. Your mother was so proud of you we could hardly stand it."

She lifted one shoulder. "Sorry about that."

"Hey, just kidding. We're all proud of you." He glanced through the plate glass that separated the sparsely furnished lounge from a small parking lot. "And we sure miss your mother. She was something else, wasn't she?" He turned back to Bella, assuring her with a nod. "In a good way."

"She was the best nurse Indian Health ever had."

"She sure was."

"She could have been a doctor." It was something she'd always thought, but she couldn't remember saying it out loud before, giving due credit, open admiration. She'd felt it, but she hadn't said it within range of her mother's ear. What kind of range did Ladonna Primeaux's hearing have now?

"She was a damn good nurse."

"Yes, she was." *But she could have been a doctor.* She'd said so herself, many times. What she'd never said was that she'd had a child to feed. "I ran into Ethan the other night."

"Where?"

"In a bar," Bella said, an answer that clearly surprised Logan. "Rapid City. I live there now."

"I watch you all the time on TV." He lifted one shoulder. "Well, not every day, but whenever I watch the news."

She smiled. It was good to be watched and even better to be acknowledged. She owed him something in return. "Ethan's following in your footsteps."

"How's that?"

"Training horses. He mentioned the wild horse training competition. He says he's going to win the big prize."

"I hope he does. Help him make a fresh start. Hope he's not spending too much time in the bars." He glanced away. "I haven't seen much of Ethan since, uh…"

"Since he went to prison?"

"He told you about that?"

"He didn't have to," she said quietly.

Logan gave a mirthless chuckle. "Made the news all the way out to California, did it?"

"The news is what the media makes it, and I'm part of the media now. I know these things." She smiled. "All we talked about was high school and what we're doing these days. He gives you credit for raising him to be a cowboy."

"A cowboy? That's down to his older brother, Trace. Although outside the rodeo, I'd say Ethan's the better hand when he's of a mind to be. They're both good, mind you, but Trace goes in for a wild ride, and Ethan…well, he's wild enough on his own."

"He was drinking iced tea."

"In a *bar?*" Apparently even more surprising.

Bella nodded. "Straight iced tea."

"I saw him at the Double D earlier this summer," Logan recalled. "First time in two years. Said he was entering the training competition. Said he was working for a rehab program."

"He told me he was a ranch hand. Square One Ranch. Something like that."

"Square One?" His tone put the news on par with tea in a bar. "That's a program for kids in trouble. Hell, that's right outside Rapid City. I didn't know he was living that close by. He didn't, uh…" Logan's wan smile spoke of a father's discomfort with being the last to know. "He didn't say."

"I thought it was a cattle ranch. That's interesting." What was left out was always more interesting than what was said. Bella added it to her mental file marked *Ethan*. Also interesting was the way she'd filed him under his first name.

Maybe because it was an old file. She was just realizing how far back it went and how carefully she'd kept it up. No surprise that he'd joined the army after he graduated. No surprise that he'd been gone awhile and come back home. No word of his military experiences, which was also no surprise. The return to Indian Country was never questioned. But he hadn't stayed around long, and the next Ethan Wolf Track news flash had been surprising. *Dirt sells,* he'd said, and if she'd been a little further along in her career, she might have tried to track him down. Not because he was in trouble—no surprise there, either. Not because the story involved a woman—most of Ethan's stories undoubtedly involved women. But there was an odd political connection.

Ethan Wolf Track and a senator's daughter? Now that was interesting. And Bella would have bet her new mobile phone that what was left out was far more interesting than what was reported.

"He's pretty sensitive about Senator Garth, isn't he?" she asked.

"Couldn't say." Staring out the window at a young couple getting into a pickup with a washing machine in the bed, Logan didn't blink. No sensitivity there. "Ethan spent two years in prison for taking Garth's car. His daughter was the one who took it, but she wouldn't stand up for him. I'd say he was sensitive about *her,* but I'd just be guessing." He turned to give Bella a what're-you-gonna-do look. "Too damn stubborn for his own good."

"He said he worked over at the Double D when he was a kid."

"Couple of summers, yeah. Like I say, Ethan's a good worker. I'll bet he's real good with those kids in the Square One program."

Bella wondered why Logan seemed so clueless

about his son. If she were still alive, Ladonna Primeaux wouldn't be betting or guessing, she would be
asking. On the other hand, Bella herself wasn't exactly being subtle about fishing for clues about the
man's family, and he was trusting her with what few
he had.

A twinge of guilt pushed her to switch tracks.

"The Double D took some grazing land away from
a neighboring rancher, didn't they? I know some of it
was public land, but wasn't there a Tribal lease, too?"

"Yep." Logan smiled. He liked this topic. "We
decided the Wild Horse Sanctuary took precedence.
The Lakota are horse people."

"But Senator Garth has a longstanding friendship
with Dan Tutan, who is—"

"My wife's father." His smile broadened. "We just
got married. Haven't told Ethan yet."

"So, uh…"

"Whose side am I on? The horses' side. So's my
wife. I haven't heard any objections from the senator.
What's he gonna do? The Tribal Council determines
how the land will be used nowadays. It's called self-
determination."

"That term is so twentieth century," Bella teased.

"Yeah, well, some of us go back that far."

"All of us do. The whole relocation program and
termination of reservations policy in the 1950s, and
then the switch to Indian self-determination in the
1970s, seems like it was only yesterday." She smiled.

"We studied it in our high school history class. Ethan sat behind me."

He laughed. "Now that must've been interesting."

"It was unsettling." She folded her arms beneath her breasts and held on tight as she glanced away. "What was interesting was twentieth-century American Indian history and how we're supposed to finally have a say over what we do with our lives. And our land." And the fact that Ethan remembered the mole on the back of her shoulder.

Bella shifted her stance, cleared her throat and her thoughts, and turned back to the Lakota leader. "So you don't think the senator can interfere with the Wild Horse Sanctuary? He sits on a couple of key committees."

"Let him sit."

"I was thinking of doing a story." He gave her a look that that reinforced his suggestion. If the story had to do with Garth, she was wasting her time. She gave a diffident shrug. "Maybe a series on the Tribe's involvement with the Wild Horse Sanctuary."

"Involvement?"

"In a good way," she added hastily.

"Kind of a *feel-good* story about Indians and horses? That always works. Sally'll take all the TV spots she can get. You know Sally Drexler—I mean Sally Night Horse—is the woman behind the whole program. You talk about a white tornado…"

He chuckled. "That's from an old TV commercial. White tornado."

"Must've been before my time."

"Mine, too. Even before self-determination, but around here some things are as timeless as Indians on horses. Especially now that you've got YouTube." He grinned. "So I say go for it. If you need me, I'm in."

"Thank you." She smiled. "Actually, it wouldn't be for KOZY-TV News. My suggestions there fall on deaf ears. They hand me an assignment, and I make it happen. Whether it means anything to anyone…" She glanced away, gave her head a little shake and turned back to a man who was known for having good ears. "That's what I was doing at the bar the other night. I was looking for different types of singles' hangouts. The place is called the Hitching Post. Doesn't that sound like a place to connect?"

"Depends on your idea of hitching, I guess. Never really got the hang of hangin' out. But Ethan…" He shrugged. "I don't know, Bella. If you're asking me about—"

"I'm not," she said quickly. But she *had* asked, and she shouldn't have. "I only meant to say that I'd run into him. You know, just saying."

"Not telling." He smiled indulgently. "Just saying."

"Do you know anything about Square One? Is it a good program?"

"It's pretty new, but they're building a good reputation. We've had some kids placed there through Tribal Court."

"Why don't we go out there and take a look? You haven't seen much of Ethan lately, and I'm looking for connections."

"I'm not much of a connection, Bella. I don't think Square One qualifies as a singles' hangout, and I don't qualify as a single. My wife's coming home for good pretty soon. The army's letting her go."

"Her choice?"

"Yeah." Again he grinned, but this time it was purely for personal pleasure. "I'm gonna be a father again."

"Congratulations. Wow." Apparently he'd wasted no time. "So how about it? Do you have some time today?"

"I do, but if Ethan's there, I'm not gonna show up uninvited. He only let me visit him once when he was in prison. Took me off his visitors list after that."

"Why would he do that?"

Logan shook his head. "I married his mother, and he took to me right away. After she left, he was different. For a while we thought sure she'd come back. His brother and I did, anyway, but Ethan never asked about her. Never jumped for the phone the way Trace did, never expected any more from her. He kinda became his own little man, you know? He got a little older, he tried to find his father. We didn't have much to go on, so it didn't pan out. Far as I know."

"You helped him?"

"Did what I could. He had a picture and the little bit his mother told him. The guy was part Indian. Don't know where he was from, though. Ethan looks a lot like the guy in the picture. I don't know what would've happened if we'd found him."

"Ethan didn't seem like one to dwell on the past. History didn't interest him all that much."

Logan smiled wistfully. "Don't let him fool you. He's as smart as they come." He punctuated a cocked finger with the cluck of his tongue. "Ethan's your connection to Square One."

Without a GPS Bella would have missed the turn-off to Square One Ranch. The sign stood so low to the ground that the dancing heads of the tall crested wheat grass obscured the small print. *Rebuilding Our Lives From the Ground Up.* The two visible roofs turned out to be a hulking old barn and a spanking-new two-story box. It wasn't until the access road took a dip that she saw the small ranch-style house that had to be a good place to start searching for someone in charge of the operation.

An attractive young blonde opened the front door before Bella mounted the steps. Bella knew the routine. Country dwellers saw visitors coming a mile off. At half a mile they had the vehicle categorized—known or unknown, in- or out-of-state, on target or gone astray. In good weather they met you outside.

In bad weather they opened the door just enough to check you out with eyes that challenged your motivation, not to mention your common sense.

But Bella had an advantage. "I've seen you on TV." The woman offered a handshake. "Shelly Jamison."

"Bella—"

"Primeaux, right? You're even prettier in person."

"Thank you. I'm aiming for professional."

"You've hit that target, too, but my observation stands." Shelly tucked her hands into the back pockets of her jeans. "What can I do for you?"

"Show me around and tell me about your program."

"You think we might be newsworthy?"

"I met with a councilman from my reservation. He suggested I come out and take a look."

"Tribal Courts have sent us a few kids since we started the program." The hands came out of the back pockets and the arms were quickly folded up front. "We haven't had any complaints."

"And you still don't." Bella shaded her eyes with one hand so she could offer an unsquinty smile. "Councilman Wolf Track said you were doing a good job here."

"Wolf Track? We've got a Wolf Track on the payroll here." Shelly glanced toward the weathered barn as her shoulders relaxed and dropped a full two inches. "Hell of a good worker."

"Ethan," Bella supplied. "I went to school with him."

"He can't be on the Tribal Council, can he? He hasn't been…I mean, he keeps busy around here, like, 24/7."

"His father's the councilman."

"He never mentioned that. You don't think that's why we get…I mean, we didn't hire Ethan as a favor to any—"

"His father didn't know he was working here. Really, I'm not here to, um, dig up any dirt." Recalling Ethan's words, Bella almost smiled. "KOZY loves a feel-good story, and I thought we might find one here. Ethan has been—"

"I know where he's been." Shelly grabbed a chunk of hair that had strayed from her low ponytail and hooked it behind her unadorned ear. "You tell anyone who asks, Ethan Wolf Track is doing just fine. The boys really look up to him. Tell the truth, he's quickly becoming indispensable around here."

"I'm not here on any kind of assignment. I've heard only good things." Bella followed the direction of Shelly's gaze toward the hulking barn. Noisy swallows darted in and out the tiny doors of the clay row houses tucked under the edge of the gambrel roof. "I'm interested in the wild horse part of your program, and I thought maybe I could take a tour." She lifted her shoulder. "And if Ethan's around, I'd like to say hello."

"Oh, he's around. Dependable as they come, that guy."

Bella smiled. "If anyone asks, I'll relay the message."

"I don't know anything about Ethan's family." Shelly stepped down to ground level, putting them on par, height-wise. "It's just that good help is hard to find when you're paying in hot dogs and beans."

"There must be other rewards," Bella prompted.

"You get to be around wild things. Wild kids, wild horses and what's left of wild country." Shelly moved into the shade of a tall cottonwood, and Bella followed suit. "Wild hearts attract each other."

"How's yours?"

Shelly grinned. "I'm the maypole they all get to dance around. I have to crunch the numbers and find the wherewithal."

"I like that image. This could be a good story, and KOZY isn't the only media outlet I can access." Bella smiled. She didn't mind throwing her TV connection into her pitch. Most people—local people, anyway—were dazzled by it. If they had nothing to hide they eventually opened their doors. Sometimes they couldn't resist even if they *did* have something to hide. Besides, everything she was saying was true. "Do you have time to show me around?"

Of course Shelly did.

She led the way with a "follow me," and they started toward the barn. "The bunkhouse is new."

She pointed toward what might have passed for a truncated no-name roadside motel—plain white, no-frills. "Kitchen and commons area downstairs, bunks upstairs. You wanna see inside? Nobody's there now except the cook."

Bella shook her head. "Another time. Who paid for the improvements?"

"We qualified for a government grant and scored some private funding, as well. We get community support, too. People come in and teach whatever skills they have to offer." Shelly glanced over her shoulder. "TV reporting must require all kinds of skills."

"You mean, besides talking to the camera?"

"Are you kidding? You're talking to thousands of people."

"I don't think of it that way," Bella said absently as they rounded the corner of the bunkhouse and headed toward the barn.

"I'd be shaking in my boots and tripping over my tongue," Shelly said.

"You get used to it. The scary part can be trying to get information out of people who don't want to talk or pictures of things they don't want you to see."

"We tell the kids, once you find out what a relief it is to come clean, you'll never want to—" They turned another corner and ran into an old flatbed farm truck with its hood up, one guy standing and another guy squatting next to the front tire, and one pair of boots sticking out from under the orange cab.

"Did you guys run over somebody?" Shelly called out. She glanced back at Bella and nodded toward the two faces now turned their way. "There's your man." She raised her voice. "You've got a visitor, Wolf Track."

"You patted her down, didn't you?" Ethan wiped his hands on a rag as he rose to his feet. "Was she packin'?"

"Packing what?" Shelly asked.

"A .38." Grinning at Bella, he touched the brim of his straw cowboy hat in salutation. "Smith & Wesson, right?"

Bella's eyes widened as she and Shelly approached the truck. "That was you?"

"You saw the pickup that cruised past? That was trouble."

"You followed me?"

"Trouble followed you. I followed *them*." Beneath the bent brim of his hat a smile danced in his dark eyes. "You don't wanna tip your hand out on the street like that, Bella. Some people might find a Smith & Wesson even more tempting than a Bella Primeaux."

She returned a level stare. "Neither one was there for the taking. As I said, I know how to use it."

"If you really knew how to use it, you wouldn't be giving away your advantage by broadcasting it."

"This sounds like an interesting reunion," Shelly injected, amused. "I'm guessing high school sweethearts."

"No. Never." Bella laughed. "I was a lowly underclassman when Ethan was the cock of the walk."

"The *what?*" Ethan said.

"You were the captain of everything except the cheerleading squad."

"And our little two-man history team." He winked at her, and she wondered whether the gesture had become pure reflex. "I dropped the ball on that one. It was your leadership that got us on the A list."

"Well played, captain. Credit your teammates. We'd love to hear a play-by-play. Sounds like the makings of an excellent lesson in humility." Shelly slipped an arm around Bella's waist. "Please stay for supper so the boys can watch their hero recover whatever he's fumbled."

"Thank you, I will." Bella gave Ethan a sweet smile. "I'm interested in seeing how a cock walks the straight and narrow walk. We already know how he talks the talk."

"You *do* know a cock is a rooster, right?" Ethan said.

"Of course. My mother had one. Beautiful plumage. But the hens got tired of him, and the neighbors complained about the crowing." She shrugged. "So we ate him. I made a tiny dance bustle out of his tail for my little cousin."

It took a moment, but Ethan burst out laughing. The boy standing near the truck joined in, and the one underneath called out, "Whoa!"

"Are you watching what you're doing there?" Still chuckling, Ethan returned to his duty. "Has the oil finished draining from the filter?"

"How am I supposed to tell?"

"Use your eyes, Dempsey. See anything dripping?"

"Out of the *filter,* Dempsey, not your face," the other boy jeered as Dempsey scooted out from under the cab.

Ethan tapped the scoffer's barrel chest. "You're not gonna make it as a comedian, so you'd better learn to make yourself useful for something else." He reached through the cab window and drew out a box. "Step two."

"I gotta get back under there?" Dempsey whined.

"What do you say, Bongo?" Ethan laid a hand on the big boy. "You wanna do the oil filter?"

Bongo chuckled as he glanced under the hood. "Does it go on top?"

"No, you gotta get down and dirty."

Dempsey laughed. "Good luck gettin' him back out."

"So that was our automotive program," Shelly said to Bella as she turned her toward the barn. "The next stop on our press tour will be the henhouse. One of the few centers of serious, steady, no-bull productivity on the place. Besides the kitchen, where we have another woman in charge. I swear, Bella, the testosterone…" With a smug smile she glanced back. "Carry on, boys."

Ethan looked up at Bella as he sank down, butt to boot heels. "You stay for supper, me and the boys'll show off our table manners. We just learned that passing is our first option."

"Yeah, but Bongo still wants to run with the bowl."

"Shut up, Dempsey," Bongo called out from under the orange cab.

"Count me in, Shelly," Bella said, amused, hesitant to move on. "I'm really interested in your program." To be honest, she felt favored, much the way she had the day Ethan had tapped her on the shoulder in history class and pointed his finger in her direction and then his own. *You're with me on this one.*

"I'm interested in her .38," Dempsey said, loud enough to be heard.

"Jeez, Dempsey, what's wrong with you?" Bongo asked.

"You *do* know a .38 is a gun."

"Sure, I do. And I figure she can read the No Firearms sign out at the gate. You're just rude, Dempsey. Ahh!" Bongo kicked both legs in the air. "Something's dripping on me!"

Ethan tipped his head and leaned to one side. "Is it hot?"

"No, but it don't taste too good."

Dempsey leaned back against the truck and howled.

"Maybe you'd better keep your mouth shut and get done, Bongo," Ethan said. "I gotta get cleaned up for supper."

Folding dining tables flanked a large pass-through window that separated the kitchen from the commons area. Two worn sofas, a card table, a TV and a few chairs furnished the opposite end of the great room. The setup was a small version of the commons at the Indian boarding school Bella had attended before her mother decided she should come back home and go to little Sinte High School. It was not Bella's choice—the South Dakota mission school had a good reputation for preparing kids for college—and she remembered questioning her mother's judgment, even accusing her of being selfish, which had turned out to be true. Her mother jealously guarded those years, claimed them as *her* time. But what she really meant was *their* time, and Bella had had no idea how short the time would be.

She wondered how many of the two-dozen boys who lined up at the window and came away with plates loaded with meat and potatoes would be taken home by their parents if and when the state stepped aside. They behaved like the boys she'd gone to school with, jostling for position, be it in suckling, pecking or batting order. Dying to get noticed, an expression a few of them would take literally if they found no other way. But here they were allowed to be boys while they learned to be men. If they could, and if they would. She'd reported on more than a few who did not.

"You really are their hero," Bella noted after Bongo and Dempsey had taken the long way around the tables to congratulate Ethan for "scoring."

"Yeah, they think I'm bad," he said with a smile.

"Which is good."

"In their eyes, maybe. Should I leave it at bad, or should I admit to a generous helping of stupid?" He shook his head as he cast a glance at the fluorescent fixture overhead. "I don't know, Bella. I'm new at this job, and I'm kinda wingin' it. You never know what's gonna work with these gangsters."

"They don't seem like gangsters."

"A couple of them are here because they won't go to school. They'd rather sit in a hole and smoke weed." He scanned the tables behind her. "Some have done worse."

"What's worse than throwing away your best chance to climb out of a weedy hole?"

"How long have you been reporting the news? You tell me."

She drew a deep breath as she ran down her mental list. She'd interviewed hardheads in all shapes and sizes. "Throwing away your next best chance on top of the first."

"Which is why they're back to Square One. It's a good option for kids who are open to this kind of rural life."

"Is it good for you?"

"It's perfect for me. Tailor-made." She gave him an incredulous look, and he laughed. "No, I'm serious. I've got a place to stay, but I'm free go. I get to eat and sleep and shower whenever I feel like it. I'm doing something useful, and they pay me for it. Plus, they let me keep a horse here." He winked at her. "I'm makin' progress."

She poked at her mashed potatoes with her fork. "I went to Sinte this morning to do a little research."

"Research?"

She nodded without looking up. "I spoke with your father."

"If you're interested in horse training, Logan's your man."

"I'm interested in the story *behind* the horses."

"How much time you got?" He gave her a sly grin. "Some 'tails' are longer than others."

It wasn't much of a joke, but the way his eyes sparkled, she had to reward him with a laugh.

"And some kicks are harder on the gut than others," he added, the sparkle fading. "So watch yourself, okay?"

The smile fell from her face. "Are you talking about Logan?"

"I'm talking about poking around behind the horse. I'm talking about being in the wrong place at the wrong time with the wrong questions." He sipped his coffee, studying her over the rim of the cup. He set it down slowly. "With all this interest in sleeping dogs and horses' asses, have you thought about doing something useful?"

"Like what?"

He frowned briefly. "Maybe go back to school for veterinary medicine."

She laughed. "You know, I never had a dog, and I've never really ridden a horse."

"No lie?"

"I try not to do that, either. So I bet you're thinking, an Indian girl who's never had a dog? No way."

"I'm thinking, a girl who's never been on a horse? That is heartbreaking."

"I didn't say I'd never been *on* one. I got on, got scared, had a very short ride."

"End of story?"

"Well, I've always loved horse stories, but you get up there, and the horse raises his head right away and starts prancing around, and you're so high off the ground…" She could almost feel the prickly tummy-to-toes *whoosh* just thinking about it. "I was six years old. That was my one chance, and I blew it."

"Stick with me, Indian girl." He cocked a forefinger at her. "I'm all about second chances." He smiled. "You want one?"

She stared at him. She knew that come-on look, the charismatic smile, the reflexive wink—she'd seen it all, generally directed at someone else. But she'd only been favored a time or two, and her adolescent self had yearned for *once more, Ethan. Look at me that way again, and I'll follow you anywhere.*

Thank God he hadn't. She would be in a fine mess now, wouldn't she?

"Tomorrow's my day off," he said. "Come back in the afternoon and let me take you riding."

"Today was *my* day off."

"That's right," he recalled. "They don't pay you to dig."

"They do, but only in certain places. They're called *assignments*. I'm very good about getting my assignments done before I go back to digging in more fertile—" she demonstrated, sinking splayed fingers into air serving as ground "—loamy ground, dark and loaded with secrets. In my business, there is no right or wrong question, only true or false answers."

"Ask me no questions, I'll tell you no..." His smile was slight, almost sad. "Truth is, I've got no answers. I'm still looking."

"My mother told me once that she was taught not to ask questions, but eventually she decided it was no good to hang back." She sat back in her chair, listening in her mind's ear, reciting word for word.

"'We live in a world full of people who love to give answers. They might not be generous with anything else, but they have answers to spare. If you don't ask, they think you're not interested. And if you're not interested…'"

"I'm interested. I'm asking." His smile turned inviting. "Would you like to go out with me sometime?"

"What time tomorrow afternoon?"

"Whenever you get off work."

"I have some flexibility in my schedule. I could try to move some things around." She pulled her woolen shoulder bag into her lap and fished out her phone. "What's your cell number?"

"I don't have one."

"So you don't have a phone number?"

"No numbers." Ethan looked straight into her eyes and gave the two words—*true* words—a moment to sink in. They were heavy enough to crush her *no wrong questions* theory. And then he smiled. "I'll be here all afternoon. Come when you can." He smiled slowly. "Just call out my name."

Chapter Three

Bella's interview with the chairman of the Rapid City Autumn Art Festival had gone well. Carson Watts described the juried competition and made a point of mentioning several of the Native artists by name. The city was gaining a reputation for galleries and shops specializing in American Indian art, and the annual festival in the fall rivaled the one that marked the beginning of tourist season in early June.

Of course, holding the art show the same weekend as Pumpkin Fest didn't hurt, Watts admitted. You had your pumpkin catapult and your beer garden with the oompah band going full tilt downtown, while the east end of Main Street hosted the more "genteel" residents and visitors. What he hadn't said—but she knew—was that his brother-in-law was the head honcho of the pumpkin party, and his own wife had chosen chairmanship of her brother's quilt show committee over her regular fund-raising assignment for the art festival. Bella had interviewed the Pumpkin Fest planners earlier in the week. They'd had her cameraman sampling German beer and opining on brands of bratwurst. She had laughed off the offer of beer for breakfast and thought better of telling the friendly group how much she hated bratwurst.

With the community celebrations covered, Bella had convinced her producer to let her take a look at the Double D Wild Horse Sanctuary for a possible story about the training competition, which would come to an end in another few weeks with some kind of performance. She was reminded that a story about the competition had been aired and that it would make sense for the same reporter to do a follow-up.

Or maybe it didn't really matter.

Go ahead, Bella. And since the wild horse place isn't too far from the reservation, why don't you check with your sources there? See if there's anything interesting going on.

She would take that as an assignment.

Her car rumbled over the cattle guard at the gate to the Double D Wild Horse Sanctuary. It had once been a cattle ranch, and she passed a few Herefords grazing alongside their white-faced black calves as she sped down the gravel access road toward an imposing white house. Upon closer inspection the place became less imposing. It was big, but the white paint needed refurbishing. The Office sign told her the house was more than a home, and the wiry old cowboy standing on the porch looked like a fixture worth investigating.

He rattled down the front porch steps on bowed legs, pumping his elbows like a flightless chicken as Bella approached. She read *Where have I seen you?* in his eyes and cheerfully introduced herself. She enjoyed being recognized.

"I'm looking for one of the *D*'s—whichever Drexler sister is in charge today."

"No more Drexlers. We got Night Horse and Beaudry, but no Drexler. Both girls are married now."

Bella smiled. "Are you Night Horse or Beaudry?"

"Me? No. Gosh, no, not me." Blushing, the little man adjusted his straw cowboy hat and did a little boot scoot in the dirt. "Them girls are like my own kin. Hoolihan's the name." He stuck out his hand. "Everybody calls me Hoolie. The girls are around here somewhere. Pretty sure Sally's over by..." He nodded toward the barn. "Here, let me show you."

Bella followed the old cowboy, whose friendly chatter reached the ears of a lovely blonde, who appeared in the open doorway leaning heavily on a sturdy cane with a tripod base. The woman shaded her eyes with her free hand and then flashed a huge smile.

"Well, I'll be damned. The paparazzi have finally tracked me down."

Bella recognized the former Sally Drexler from the original KOZY interview. The new last names would come naturally soon enough.

"Where's your camera, Miss Primeaux?" Sally laughingly demanded as she emerged from the barn. "I'm ready for my close-up."

"What've you done now, girl?" Hoolie chided. "I told you, my film star days are over, so don't be signing me up for any more of them promotional videos."

"You're our most authentic-looking relic of the Old West, Hoolie." Sally turned to Bella as she pulled off her work gloves. "You do a story on the Double D, you get Hoolie in the picture for free. For a donation, he comes with woolly chaps." She offered a handshake. "Sally Night Horse." She glanced at Hoolie, grinning. "I love saying that. *Sally Night Horse.*" To Bella she added, "We're newlyweds."

"Not me," said Hoolie.

"Hoolie turned me down years ago," Sally said. "You KOZY people sure are quick. I just sent the email this morning."

"What email?"

"You know, where it says *Got news? Contact us.* I told them they oughta be setting something up for the grand finale of our training competition." Sally patted Bella's shoulder. "And here you are. My favorite reporter, too."

Bella frowned. "My producer didn't say anything about an email."

"Thought of it on her own, did she? I'm sure glad she didn't give it to the guy who came out here before. He didn't know a mustang from a unicorn. Have a seat." Sally gestured toward a wooden bench on the shady side of the barn and then proceeded to beat Bella to the far end of it.

Bella hesitated. Whatever physical strength the woman lacked, she more than made up for in vitality and sheer will. She seemed to fill up more than physical space. She had considerable personal presence.

"Come on, take a load off. Mine's heavier than yours, so humor me." Sally patted the empty space beside her. "Sit down and tell me what you need. We've got pictures, we've got stories, we've got facts and figures. It's been one hell of a ride, and we haven't even gotten to the best part yet. I mean, *I* have, but that's because I've met my soul mate. And I've only nibbled around the edges of that discovery. The ride gets better and better. There's so much more we can do here."

"I'd better get to haulin' that hay," the old cowboy muttered, edging away.

"Are you blushing, Hoolie?"

"It's my farmer tan." He lifted his cowboy hat. He was ruddy below the eyebrows, pale and polished on top. "It ends right here. See? Don't you be signing me up for any stories with pictures, Big Sister." He replaced his hat and tugged at the brim in deference to their visitor as he backpedaled a step or two. "Never know what you're gonna say."

"I'm just sayin' it's all good." Eyes dancing, Sally glanced at Bella. *Between girls.* "And I'm still looking forward to handing over that twenty-thousand dollars to the winning trainer. Thank God I'm not judging. I've been getting pictures from the trainers. You should see some of the riders they've lined up to show the horses. You wanna show us a gentle horse, you put a kid in the saddle, right?" Sally took a deep breath and glanced heavenward. "I need more prizes."

"Maybe I could help you get some. Show me some of your pictures and I can find a way to use them. We do community support spots all the time."

"We'll take some of those." Sally nodded. "But what I really want you to cover is the competition. Show off the horses and the people coming from all over. If I had to make a choice…"

"Maybe we can do both. It doesn't hurt to try."

"I wanna show you around." Sally balanced her weight on the cane and levered herself off the bench. "The best view is from the back of a horse, but I need to rest up first for that."

"Start with the pictures," Bella suggested as she sprang to her feet. She wouldn't offer help unless she was asked, but she was ready. And, yes, she was also ready to ask a little and offer to listen a lot. "Tell me more about your program," she said as they headed for the house. "How you got started, what it takes to create a sanctuary. Talk to me about how you get the land you need and cooperation from all the bureaucrats that would have to be involved with something like this. And your neighbors. You must have some helpful neighbors. Not everyone wants a wildlife sanctuary butting up against their pasture."

Sally moved like a woman living in a body that couldn't keep up with her mind. Bella had seen the same frustration in her mother, and it scared her a little. Not the hint of impatience—she understood that—but the reality. It was a feeling she tucked away, to be studied later.

"Come on inside," Sally told Bella when they reach the top of the porch steps. She nodded toward a wheelchair parked beside a porch swing. "On days when the saddle's out of reach, that's my ride. MS." She reached for the screen door. "You know, multiple sclerosis. The last guy KOZY sent out was here for about ten minutes. One look at me, and he was after a whole different story. He wanted to put me in my wheelchair out in the corral, gather some horses around me and then mike me up. That's what he said. And you know what I said?"

"I know what *I* would have said."

Sally laughed. "And that's what I said, too. Not to

mention, that chair is camera shy." She led the way through an old-fashioned foyer and nodded toward the first door past the foot of the staircase. "But I know a slacker from a doer. Glad they decided not to send a boy to do a woman's job this time."

The door led to an office whose walls were covered with pictures of horses—all sizes, colors, attitudes and settings. The heart of the matter. Sally probably spent more time in this room than she wanted to, so she brought her outdoor world inside. This was the Double D's hub. Her regular desk chair was probably the one sitting on the porch, but there were a couple of padded folding chairs and a daybed, lots of room to roll around, a desktop computer, file drawers and desk trays galore, and an array of framed family photographs standing on shelves above.

Sally took a shot of a foursome down from the shelf. "This is Hank and me with my sister, Ann, and her new husband, Zach. This was taken at their wedding. Hank was the soloist, and I was the maid of honor. That was just last spring." She flashed Bella a smile as she reached for another shot of four smiling faces. "And here's *my* wedding picture. We work fast here. You know this guy." She pointed to Logan Wolf Track. "He married my BFF Mary Tutan just a little over a month ago. Double wedding." She looked up, eyes dancing. "Me and Hank figured what the hell? Everyone else is doing it."

"It doesn't look like that's what anybody in this picture was thinking," Bella said of the four glowing faces. She glanced into a frame on the shelf above the wedding pictures.

"That's Trace Wolf Track," Sally said, indicating the man on the bucking horse. "Logan's adopted son." She took the picture down from the shelf. "You know him? Rodeo cowboy."

"I went to school with his brother."

"You know Ethan? He's one of our contestants. He's even better looking than this guy, if you can believe that. Have you seen him lately? He's like—"

"I met with Logan recently over at the Tribal Office," Bella said, sparing the shot of Trace Wolf Track in action little more than a glance. She knew how to learn a lot by asking only a little, but it wasn't a two-way street. Seeing Ethan would not enter into this conversation. She was keeping that close. "Indian Country is one of my beats whenever my producer thinks there might be something newsworthy going on."

"Logan's been a big help to the sanctuary," Sally said. "Backed us on leasing some Tribal land, which gave us a leg up on getting a big tract of public land adjacent to the reservation. We'll be able to take on a lot more horses."

Bella set Logan's older son back on the metaphorical shelf. Now she was getting somewhere. "Your neighbor was running cattle on that land, wasn't he? Dan Tutan?"

"Damn tootin' he was. Poor guy's losin' it." Sally laughed. "In more ways than one."

"What do you mean?"

"I don't know, he's just…" Sally snapped a lever on her cane and telescoped it closed. "To all intents and purposes he lost his daughter, Mary, a long time ago, but now that she's married to Logan, the plot thickens."

"How so?"

"Let's just say ol' Dan better start tootin' a sweeter tune or he won't be bouncing that first grandbaby on his knee. Of course, if I get to be godmother—which I'm counting on—he'll have to go through me no matter what."

Sally hadn't told Bella anything she didn't already know, but a baby brother or sister for Ethan seemed like a pretty big deal. Since Logan and Mary had just gotten married and Logan had said he hadn't seen much of Ethan, she wondered if he knew. Or cared.

And why did she wonder or care whether Ethan cared? She was looking for a story about Indian land and Dan Tutan's good friend Senator Garth. Ethan Wolf Track figured in somewhere out on the fringe at best.

"Is everything signed and sealed on the leases?" Bella asked. "I mean, I've heard you might have some opposition."

"Just Tutan, but the Tribal Council already shot him down."

"Tutan has influential friends in Washington. One, anyway."

"Who?"

"Senator Perry Garth. I just wondered if you'd actually gotten anything on paper."

Bella read the message in Sally's eyes. *Of course I'm dotting the i's.*

"The leases turn over in November," Sally said. "I don't care who Tutan's cozy with. D.C.'s a world away. The people I deal with at the regional Bureau of Land Management office, the ones who handle wild horse issues, they tell me renewal's in the bag. They need this sanctuary. They've got no place to put the horses they consider unadoptable. That's what we do. We give them a home where they can roam." Sally's grin was infectious. "You know, with the deer and the antelope. No buffalo. Wish I had some. Hank would love that. I don't suppose you've met my husband, Hank?"

"I don't think so."

"He's not from this reservation, but he has connections here. In fact, I think his father worked for Tutan some years ago, but I don't know much about that. We haven't talked much about... Did I tell you we got married at the Tribal building? In the judge's chambers. It was so cool. No fuss at all, just *bam.*" Sally slapped the back of her hand into her palm.

"Man and wife. Love it." She smiled. "I don't think Tutan's gonna give us any trouble. I think he's afraid of Hank."

Fear. Could be something... "Why?"

"They've had words. I don't know exactly what those words were, but they weren't friendly." Sally took another picture down from the shelf. Two young women—Sally and someone in an academic robe. "It wasn't so long ago that it was just my sister, Ann, and me running the place. We had Hoolie and a few high school kids working for us, some volunteers helping out. Then Zach Beaudry came along. Another rodeo cowboy. Have you heard of him?"

Bella shook her head. Rodeo itself held no interest for her, but she knew better than to show it. Listening—her strong suit—had always served her well. Talkers like Sally tended to ramble, dropping crumbs of information along the way. With any luck Sally would wander back and pick up the tidbit about Hank's father working for Tutan. Even if she didn't, Bella had sniffed the crumb and made a mental note of the scent.

"My husband works the rodeo circuit as a medic, so that's how he knew Zach." Sally perched on the edge of the big desk. "Life's funny, isn't it?" she went on. "Not much happens for the longest time, and then Zach's pickup breaks down outside our gate and the Double D family starts growing." She gave a catbird's smile. "And 'Damn Tootin' isn't very popular around these parts. So I'm not worried."

"I don't know much about rodeo. The only name I know is Trace Wolf Track." And the name was clearly a connection to the horses, which were Sally's claim to the land. "Do rodeo contractors ever get hold of your mustangs?"

"First of all, they're not mine. And the people who adopt horses could use them that way, but I doubt it happens often. Good bucking stock is hard to find. You almost have to breed for it, and those animals are valuable and well taken care of, so if you're looking for some kind of scandal…" Sally's smile had gone cool. "I was a rodeo stock contractor for a short time years ago. I took good care of my animals."

"Oh, I have no doubt," Bella said quickly. "I'm interested in the making of a sanctuary, the commitment to providing at least some animals with the space to be wild. I could really get into a story like this."

Sally's eyes lit up again. "That's what I like to hear."

"But I have to convince my producer to let me do it."

"Tell your boss that first guy flat out offended me, and I don't want him back." Sally reached for a Post-it pad. "Better yet, give me the guy's name and number."

"Let me handle it." Bella reached into her shoulder bag—her ever-present office on a string—and poked around while she spoke. "You might want to check on the public lands leases. I've heard that one of their favorite tactics is to come up with a snag when it's too late to get it straightened."

"Whose tactics?"

"Bureaucrats. My mother used to say the word as though it had been soaked in sour milk." She produced a business card from her woolen bag. "If you smell anything fishy, would you call me?"

"I was gonna offer you lunch, but now..." Cautiously Sally took the card in hand. "Dead fish and sour milk?"

Bella smiled. "Damn tootin'."

Bella had called ahead, but she didn't know whether to knock on the door of the house at Square One or walk in. She hadn't seen an office sign anywhere. Or, for that matter, any sign of an office. She remembered knocking on the door of the Wolf Track home years ago, shoring up her courage with a bit of self-talk and going in search of Ethan. She'd gone over what she would say as she stood there on the front step, grateful that the log house was far enough out of town that no one would see her. Too far to walk. Too windy, too cold. Her mother was waiting in the car, keeping it running, keeping the heat on.

How did you end up with him as a partner on this

project? Why don't you just do your part and let him twist in the wind?

Because it would be incomplete. Because I'd get laughed at. Not him. Me. Because I thought we'd do this thing together.

She could almost feel her mother's angry stare boring into her back as she headed around the corner of the house. *So who're you gonna team up with next time? Not some football hero, I hope.*

Oh, yeah, the heat was on.

"I got your message."

Bella was snapped back to the present and whirled around to find that this time the heat was coming from Ethan's eyes. They'd always made her a little nervous, made her feel as though he knew more than she did. Not that what he thought was terribly important, but he was older, wiser, more experienced, and he knew things. He had answers to questions she hadn't thought of yet—at least back then.

"I said I'd come."

"I said I'd be here." He adjusted his battered straw hat by the brim and smiled. "A man of his word meets a woman of hers."

"I hope we're really going to ride horses." She stuck out her right leg. "I wore my boots." With riding heels. Guaranteed to keep her feet in the stirrups.

"Pretty flashy." He gave a nod toward the barn, and she lowered her boot—a step, she hoped, in a useful direction. "Did you buy those today?" he asked.

"Last night."

"First pair?"

"First pair of cowboy boots, yes. They're not very comfortable." She picked up her pace. One step behind was not her way.

"You gotta break 'em in."

Her boots squeaked on cue. She glanced up at him, and they both laughed.

"I paid a visit to the Double D this morning," she told him as they approached a rail fence. "I'm going to ask if I can to do a feature on the competition. I want to tie it into land use and can't-we-all-just-get-along and stuff like that." She braced her arm over the chest-high fence and turned to him. "You say you're going to win?"

"Get along with who?" he asked, ignoring her question.

"Oh, you know, the farmers and the cattlemen, the cowboys and the Indians. How can you be sure you'll win?"

He gave her an incredulous look. "Damn, woman, let it go. That is *so* past history." He bumped her arm with his elbow. "To boot, we both already passed history." He tipped his head back and laughed. "Ah, funny stuff, Bella. Wait till you see my horse. He can go from zero to sixty and stop on a dime."

She smiled. "Turning your thrill gauge upside down is he?"

"My thrill gauge?" He laughed again. "It's pretty easy to thrill me these days. I get a kick out of simply turning a knob and pushing the door open." He demonstrated with a handful of air. "All by myself."

"No hands tied behind your back?"

"That was always my brother's favorite boast." He squared his shoulders and pitched his voice down low. "*Hell, I can do that with one hand tied behind my back.* So I always wanted to go him one better."

"I'll bet *that* was some competition." Bella rested her elbows on the rail and surveyed the pasture beyond. No horses. No cattle. Just grassy hills, clear blue sky. "I read about your conviction," she said quietly. "And, no, it wasn't *big* news out where I was, but it wouldn't have been news at all if it hadn't involved a senator."

"His daughter," Ethan amended. "Politics and sex, right? The only thing missing was money."

"Money's always somewhere in the mix."

"Don't look at me." He turned his back to the fence, which positioned him for a challenging look at her. "I stole a car and a girl. No money."

"There was money somewhere, Ethan. That's where the power comes from."

"I did the crime, I did the time, and now I'm done with it."

She frowned. "You pled not guilty."

"Against the advice of my attorney. Turned out I *was* guilty." Leaning back, he glanced past her, tucked his lower lip under his front teeth and gave a deafening whistle.

Bella turned toward the sound of pounding hooves. A stout buckskin galloped toward them, his mane flapping like a black flag.

"Impressive," Bella said.

"Damn straight." Ethan betrayed his secret, opening his hand to let the horse snuffle up a tiny brown treat. "Big Boy, meet Bella. She's a reporter. She's got a ton of questions. Help me show her some answers."

"I haven't asked you anything."

"I noticed." He slid her a subtle wink. "You're good."

"Yes, I am. Are you going to show me the dime-stopping routine?"

"Nope. I'm gonna take you out riding. Watch this." Ethan climbed the fence, lured the horse into position with another treat and a little sweet talk, grabbed a fistful of mane and mounted. He grinned at Bella. "How do you like my wild mustang?"

"Amazing. How long since he was wild?"

"How long since I whistled? A minute or two?"

"He's not wild. You've tamed him."

"If I turn him out of this pasture, he'll head for the hills and his band of brothers. He won't give me another thought until I go out there and run him back in."

She nodded at the unfettered horse. "Will he do that for anyone else?"

"No one else has tried. You want to?"

She shook her head. "I want a kid horse."

"The kids are out in the field. Meet me at the gate by the barn and we'll steal their horse for an hour or so."

She watched him ride away, loping the buckskin along the fence line. Quite a picture, she thought. Both magnificent looking, neither quite tame. Together they made a story, and she could stand aside and watch and listen and make notes. She could find that story and tell it in a good way, so that people would find it and feel it and value the lives they lived at the back of beyond. She had a role to play.

And she'd said she would do the horseback-riding scene, hadn't she?

Well, at least she looked the part. She opened the appointed gate and watched Ethan swing his leg high over the buckskin's head and slide to the ground.

He grinned. *Did you see that?* And she nodded, suitably impressed. The mustang had earned another treat.

"He took to this apple-flavored stuff right away, which is kinda surprising. It's generally an acquired taste." He scratched the horse's withers. "Ain't it, Big Boy?" He glanced over the buckskin's back and peered at the bright blue horizon. "So you've really never had a look at this country of yours from the back of a horse?"

"Country of mine?"

"Isn't this part of the land Warrior Woman blogs about? The Great Sioux Nation, she says." He flashed a knowing smile. "That's you, isn't it? Warrior Woman?"

It was her blogging handle. "How did you know?"

"I'm an Indian, too, Bella. I'm not sure what tribe, but it's in my blood," he told her. And then he disappeared into the barn with the horse following him as far as the open door. Within seconds Ethan reappeared carrying a saddle on his shoulder. "I know how to read sign."

"What sign?"

"The sign that somebody wants to be waited on. Saddle rack's in here."

"I don't have a horse."

"I'll get the horse. You get the saddle." He grinned at her as she walked past him. "Together, we're gonna ride."

Half a dozen saddles were shelved on wall pegs just inside the door. "Any saddle?"

"Any saddle," was the response from outside.

She eyed the hanging array of horse headgear. "What about the other stuff?"

He appeared in the doorway.

She turned and quickly pulled down the nearest saddle. "Got one."

She thought he might take it from her—the damn thing was heavy—but he walked around her and selected two sets of headstalls with reins.

"So you use your tracking skills on the internet?" She followed him into the corral and dropped the saddle beside the one he'd brought out. "That's interesting. That's a topic worth exploring. Are you a hunter?"

"No. Never hunted. Never will. Lost my right to bear arms." He gripped the handful of tack and did a quick biceps curl. "Except these. These can go bare."

"They're quite impressive." He was wearing a gray T-shirt, and for the first time she noticed some ink peeking out from under his sleeve. On impulse she pushed his sleeve up and discovered a pair of hawks fighting in flight. "The artwork seems a little amateurish."

"You don't like that?" He glanced at it and shrugged. "Neither do I, but I'm stuck with it. Don't know what I was thinking." He offered a sheepish grin. "Literally. Nothing like a three-day bender for blowing the mind."

"Was that the first thing you did after your release from prison?"

"Hell, no. First thing I did was go around turning knobs and pushing doors open. Hold this." He handed her one of the headstalls. "Getting drunk was the first thing I did after I got discharged from the army." He spoke quietly as he approached the mustang. "And the second thing. Maybe the third thing. I lost count."

"But the army was *before*…"

"Yeah, before. But I did some stuff *between*. Check it out, Big Boy." The buckskin lowered his head and snuffled the proffered headstall. "I did road construction, worked for Logan, followed Trace around a little bit. Even took a few college classes."

"Where you met Senator Garth's daughter."

"And the rest is history." He turned to the horse. "The woman is a history freak, boy." Ethan lifted the simple, handmade-looking piece of tack over the horse's head. There was no bit to coax into his mouth. "What's past is present, they say. How're we gonna live with that, huh? You and me?" He glanced over his shoulder at her as he rubbed the horse's face. "So come on, tell me the truth. Have you really never ridden?"

"I just need a gentle, well-broke mount," she said, sidestepping the question. "Nothing fancy. No stopping on a dime or going on a tear." The closer the moment of getting on a horse came, the less she wanted to think about her long-ago but never forgotten experience.

He smiled. "I'll go wake your horse up."

"But first…" She shoved her hand in the front pocket of her jeans, pulled up the contents and flipped a glinting dime, which he caught midair. She nodded. "Prove it."

He laughed. "Yes, ma'am."

He flipped the reins over the mustang's withers, vaulted onto his bare back and put on a quick show for her. The horse leaped into action, skidded to a stop and reversed directions like a swinging door.

Bella knew little about training horses, but she was impressed. "How long have you been working with him?"

"Little over two months."

"And he was completely wild?"

"Came straight out of the hills." Ethan swung his leg over the horse's withers and slid to the ground. "Course he'd had a couple of human encounters. For one, he's a gelding. But I had no part in that, did I, Big Boy?" He patted the horse's shoulder.

"Who *did?*" she asked.

"Any doctoring these horses get is done by a vet. They try not to interfere too much when the horse is in the wild, but you need geldings for the adoption program."

Bella felt the urge to pat Big Boy, too, but she stayed put. "Did he come with the name, or did you give it to him?"

"That's just what I call him. There's gonna be an auction after the competition to benefit the sanctuary, and this guy will bring in big bucks. I figure naming rights go with him."

"And if you named him, you'd be hard-pressed to let him go."

"There's always another horse." He entreated her with a nod. "Come hold him for me."

"I don't…"

"Sure you do. You two have a lot in common. You're both observers."

She took one cautious step, then another. Ethan reached for her hand, uncurled her fingers with his thumb and drew her palm to the horse's big, soft nostril. It widened as Big Boy took her measure and found her acceptable. Ethan placed the ends of the reins in her hand.

The thing about animals smelling fear must have been an old wives' tale, Bella thought as Ethan walked away. Or maybe that was just predators. Animals driven to knock you down, step all over you and eat you alive.

"You wouldn't do that, would you, Big Boy?" she whispered. "We have that in common, too. We're gentle creatures. We eat plants."

Ethan emerged from the barn leading a small black horse. "This one's for you." He dropped the lead rope, and the horse stood patiently while he straightened the saddle pad and set the saddle.

"Does he have a name?"

"This is Sister Sara."

"She." Bella looked up and found Big Boy staring

back at her. "A mare. We like mares. They're usually gentle, aren't they?"

"This one is." Ethan brought the mare over and traded reins. He watched Bella take quiet stock of the mare's response to her. One female sizing up the other.

"Would you rather do something else?" Ethan asked.

"No. Oh, no, I've been looking forward to this. Obviously." She dug one heel into the dirt and tipped her toe toward the sky, showing off her new boots again.

"One step at a time, then. Step one is to mount up."

No problem—as long as Sister Sara didn't move. Ethan spoke to her while Bella got herself lined up, put mind over matter and pushed off. One smooth move. Victory.

"How's that feel?" Ethan asked.

She looked down at him. "So far, so good." Nobody was moving yet.

"Yeah?" He smiled. "You look good up there. You feel okay?"

"I do." Bella nodded quickly. "I do. We're steady. Nobody's nervous. This is a good start."

"Take the reins easy and find your contact point."

She felt a little jittery as she slid the leather straps through her fingers. Where was it, this contact point? Would it show the horse that she was in charge?

"Easy," he said softly, laying his hand over hers. "This isn't a lifeline. You don't hang on with these." He moved his hand to her thigh. Now she *really* felt jittery. "You hang on with these."

"I know. I know that."

He looked up and considered her face for a moment. She wasn't sure how much the hand resting on her thigh had to do with it, but her insides were all abuzz.

"Okay, just how bad was your experience?"

She lifted one shoulder. "I got dumped. Hard."

One corner of his mouth twitched. "I mean, with a horse."

"I've never been dumped by anything else." A little fake indignation calmed her nerves, and she smiled. "I got left in the lurch on a history project once, but since I landed on my feet, it doesn't qualify."

"How long is it gonna take you to forgive me for that one?" He turned to Big Boy, whispered something and reached for the top of his headstall.

"Forgiving is no problem. It's the forgetting. It just seems to jump out there when I need a good comeback. And what are you doing?"

"Turning my horse loose. I'm going with you." He slid her boot out of the stirrup, put his hand under her knee and lifted it toward the saddle swell. With a light touch on the saddle horn and a toe in the stirrup he swung up effortlessly and settled behind her. "Our Sister Sara's gonna take us both."

"She doesn't mind?"

"Doesn't seem to. Do you?" Bella shook her head. "We're just gonna amble along so you can get the feel of being safe on a horse. How's that?"

Bella nodded, and Ethan guided her foot back into the stirrup, then took the reins in his left hand and urged the horse through the gate and into a pasture that had been grazed down to crisp nubs.

"I remember sitting across from you in the library," he said, "working out the plans and looking stuff up. You were so damn serious, thought you knew it all, and if you'd been a little less bossy, maybe a little older…"

"What?" she coaxed.

"You mighta been in trouble. I remember going along for the fun of it, thinking you were way too smart, too cute, too mouthy and too young. What I don't remember is why I didn't show up that night."

She laughed uneasily. She could almost feel the inked wings of the birds on his arm fluttering against her shoulder. "*You* were serious about other things."

"I was living in the moment." He laid his free hand on her shoulder. "You know what? You need to relax. How bad were you hurt?"

"I wasn't hurt. I was mad."

"At the horse?"

"Oh, that. I broke my butt."

He laughed.

She didn't. "Hairline fracture of the coccyx."

"Oh, yeah, that hurts. Sorry. No wonder you're tense." Slowly he began kneading her right shoulder. "Let's try to loosen you up some. Let me untie this knot so you can let your arms down." He rested his chin on her left shoulder and rocked it side to side. "This side, too. Stop thinking. You don't need a comeback."

No kidding. Tight loops began opening up, raised parts lowering, hung-up pieces sinking, and, oh, it all felt good in concert.

But she wasn't about to start singing.

"Shouldn't you pay attention to the road?"

"You've got the front seat." He chuckled soft and low, his breath warm in her ear. "Lean back and take the reins. Then you'll really be in charge."

"You're making me nervous."

"Take the reins in your left hand. You can still hang on to the swells with your right. Not the horn." He touched the high pommel that anchored the saddle horn. "The swells."

"I don't want to make the horse nervous," she muttered, but she accepted the assignment.

"She's a kids horse," he whispered as he drew his hand back and slid it around her waist.

She quickly sucked in her belly and then half expected somebody to laugh at her. Who cared whether she had a waist? She was fine. She was healthy and fit. Her jeans rode her hipbones, and his hand had no business hovering around there. But it was warm and comforting, and she was pretty far out of her comfort zone. Still, with all the square inches of surface her body possessed, the only patch she felt at the moment was underneath his hand.

And then he moved it. "Lean back," he said, and he pressed her to him. "Relax and get into the flow with us." His fingers stirred. "Sister Sara ain't the nervous type, and she's got the sweetest rockin' horse lope. You wanna try it out?"

"Not yet."

"Is it me or the horse?"

She laughed a little. "It's me. I don't want to be afraid. Horses are *beautiful*."

"What about me?"

"You're beautiful, too."

"Do you want to stop being afraid of me?"

She turned her head quickly and found herself shaded by the brim of his hat and basking in the warmth of his gaze. "I'm not…"

He stopped her answer with a soft, sure kiss. Her words would have been meaningless, anyway. A hollow denial would be a waste of breath. Words stood no chance against a kiss, and his was pure and promising. She drew in the feel and the scent of him, meeting his kiss in kind.

Yes, I do.

He lifted his head and smiled down at her. "Give me time. I'll show you how."

She glanced at the horizon. Time was easy. There was nothing to it. Being together was something else.

"Talk to me," he said. He nudged the mare, and she picked up her pace. "Tell me about your college days. What was it like for you? Was it hard?"

"Very hard, and very good for me, thanks for asking."

He rested his chin on the top of her head, staking a claim. "You always talk cute when you're nervous?"

"I rarely do things that make me nervous. This is out of character for me."

"You go on TV. Most people would be shaking in their boots."

"Would you?"

"Hell, yeah. God knows what I'd say. But you never miss a beat. First time I saw you, I said, *hey, I know her.*" He chuckled. "But I didn't, did I?"

"What did you *think* you knew about me?"

"You were always one to speak your mind, but only when you had something to say. I thought down deep you were pretty shy." His hand stirred against her midriff. "Pretty. And shy."

"It's not down that deep."

"When you read about me going to prison, did you say, *hey, I know him?*" A beat passed, and then another. "If that's what makes you nervous—"

"It's not," she assured him. "I didn't say anything.

I just kept reading. One thing about not speaking up until you have something to say is that you get to hear more, maybe see more, than you would otherwise. That's how I knew you, not from something I read."

"And you liked me."

"No, I didn't. I had a crush on you, but that's not really the same thing. I was beneath your notice until you needed me to get you through a required class."

"Needed you?" He snorted. "I could've done that thing myself."

"But you didn't have to."

"And you know damn well I noticed you."

"You teased me."

"Of course I did. I was a cocky eighteen-year-old. And you were, what, fifteen? Believe it or not, I don't go around lookin' for trouble."

"That's my job."

He laughed. "You're doing just fine, Bella. Whatever hurt I caused, you rose above it. And now I'm the one who gets to polish up his image when he says, *hey, I know her.*"

"No apology for calling me Bella the Fella when one of your buddies said I needed to grow a pair?"

"Aw, jeez," he groaned. "I said that?"

"I was fifteen and flat as a board."

"What did you do? I know you didn't go home and cry."

"I threw a pencil at you, but I missed. And then I went home and grew a pair."

"A very nice pair. I noticed, Bella. I definitely noticed." He laid his free hand on her shoulder again, then rubbed it down over her arm. "You've relaxed. You notice the difference in Sister Sara? No resistance."

"I'm doing better?" She smiled. "And I'm not freaking out inside. I'd like to try it on my own." She glanced up at him. "Next time."

"We're havin' a next time?"

"I was thinking of blogging on you."

"I don't think I've ever been blogged on. I notice you're pretty good at it."

"You won't find better."

"Why don't we pull over to the side of the road and you can start now. Does it hurt the first time?"

"I'm betting you're pretty thick-skinned."

"Only in some places."

"I'll make a deal with you," she said. "Come over to the studio when you have a little time. If I'm on a story, you can tag along if you want to. And then I'll start doing you. Blog style."

"You make it sound real tempting, but I've been out of circulation for a while now. I'm what you'd call fresh fish. You throw the net over me, I'll be taking you for one crazy ride."

"Throw the net over you," she mused. "I like that. It's quotable. Where's a pencil when you need one?"

"You're still using pencils? Don't they get hung up in the net?"

"Still funny after all these years." She turned to look up at him. "With your looks and my brain, we might actually be a team this time."

"You've got looks, lady. Good looks. *Great* looks."

She flashed him a smile.

"Hey. You're supposed to say something back."

"*Of course* you have a brain, Ethan. It's all in the application."

Chapter Four

Ethan had never been to a television studio, and he didn't know what he was expecting, but it was something a little grander than the building KOZY-TV shared with a veterinary clinic and a real estate office. The station occupied the lion's share of the space, and it was flanked by an impressive tower, but the news desk was smaller than it looked on TV, and the weatherman stood in front of a solid green backdrop instead of a map. Bella called it magic. Ethan added the word *tricks*.

There were wires and cables hanging from the high ceiling and strung across the dark floor, lots of equipment on wheels, messages and images dancing on big and small screens, and two monster cameras.

The cameras looked cool. Everything else was disappointing, like shaking hands with the actor who played Ironman and realizing his hand was half the size of yours.

Bella introduced two behind-the-scenes people who showed him how their gadgets worked. It was one computer, two computer, three computer, four. "More machines, fewer bodies," the young engineer said. "The station manager says if I can grow an extra ear and another hand, I'll have a job for at least five more years." He nodded at a pretty young woman hurrying past with an armload of file folders. "But she won't."

The woman skidded to a stop, neck arched. "Won't what?"

"Marry me," the young man said.

"In your dreams, Richard."

Richard grinned as they watched her disappear bit by lovely bit down a flight of stairs. "What I could do with another hand," he said under his breath.

Bella was already moving Ethan on to the next tour stop, but he tapped the man's shoulder in passing. "Machines can't replace a man's hands, no matter what anyone on TV says."

He left Richard laughing his headphones off.

"I'll show you how we switch over from news to weather," Bella was saying as they stepped into a den of rubber snakes on the dark news set. "Hey, Paul, is Darryl here?" she asked an older man who was monkeying around with a big camera. "I want him to meet Ethan Wolf Track." She turned to Ethan. "Darryl Brugmann is the—"

"Sports guy." A bright-eyed fellow with a spiky haircut appeared with a firm handshake at the ready. "Any relation to…"

"His brother." Sports guy was a short guy. Ethan grinned. "I caught Trace's interview with you a few months ago."

"Your brother's a hell of a bronc rider. What's your event? Rodeo usually runs in the family, and you look like a bulldogger to me."

"Nope. I got no interest in wrestling a steer to the ground just to let him up again. The rodeo genes went to my brother. I got the hand-me-down over-alls." Ethan shoved his hands in the back pockets of his jeans. "I'm a workin' man. A cowboy, at least for now."

The sportscaster looked up at Bella. "Interesting. Are you doing something on cowboys? Or overalls?"

"I'm showing a friend around the studio before I go out on assignment."

"How far do you have to go? I'm covering a game tonight, and I need the new Betacam with the good tripod."

"I'll use the old camera," Bella said cheerfully. "I don't need a tripod."

"And I get John."

"I don't need John. I have a workin' man right

here." She threaded her arm though Ethan's and around his back, smiling up at him. "Right?"

"Right. You don't need John." In the face of all the fancy equipment, he felt damn good about edging John out of the picture.

"What they say about working cowboys must be true," Darryl said. "Kinda like a Swiss Army Knife." He looked Ethan up and down, checking to see whether he was the deluxe model. "Your brother sure can ride."

"He sure can." Ethan smiled. He was standing there with Bella Primeaux's arm around his waist.

Brugmann gave a snappy salute and turned on his heel. "Have fun, kids."

"You think you like somebody," Ethan mused as he watched the little man make his swaggering exit. "And then you meet him in person."

Bella smiled. "Darryl thinks he's a big fish in a small pond. The only part he's got right is the size of the pond."

"Maybe you need to stop messin' with fish and find yourself a real man." Before she could slip away, Ethan slipped his arm around Bella's shoulders and gave her an affectionate squeeze. "Not a John, though. You don't want a John." He frowned. "What does John do, anyway?"

"He's our cameraman. We're down to one. The way the station's been cutting the budget, I'm surprised *I* still have a job." She patted his midsection. "Are you any good with a camera, cowboy?"

"I can point and shoot."

"That's all I need. Otherwise I have to shoot myself."

She was walking him toward a set of stairs. He hoped they led to the great outdoors. "Sounds like your job is harder than it looks."

"It depends on the assignment, and this one could get weird. We're going to talk to a dog breeder."

Ethan stepped back and let Bella take the stairs first. "We're talkin' puppies?"

"Puppies by the cageful. An affiliate in Boston got this lead on what they think is a mill shipping puppies out east. Apparently the owner agreed to let us take a look, so maybe it's a legitimate breeder." She turned when she reached the top of the stairs. "South Dakota doesn't require a license, so legitimacy is in the eye of the beholder."

"I can't shoot puppies," he teased as he stepped onto the landing. "Sorry. That's just wrong."

"I doubt we'll get to see many puppies. If these people are the kind we think they are, I'll give you a nice reward for full-face shots of any of the people. What would you like?"

"Like a prize at the fair?" He smiled hungrily. "Something from your top shelf."

She gave him a quick lesson on the handheld video camera and loaded the necessary equipment into her car. Ethan offered to drive so that she could use the GPS on her phone to find the place, which was pretty far out in the sticks. When they got there, the gate across the access road was locked.

Bella was back on the phone. "Hello, this is Bella Primeaux from KOZY News. I have an appointment for an interview with Mrs. Mosher. The gate's locked." She lowered the phone almost instantly. "They said to wait."

"Somebody's coming." Ethan appraised the approaching vehicle. It was a Hummer, for God's sake, bearing down on Bella's angelic white Honda. A South Dakota farmer with a Hummer? "I've got a bad feeling about this, Bella."

"Welcome to my world. You never know when something interesting might turn up"

"No, this is a feeling I've had before. Many times. Same world, different neighborhoods." The Hummer pulled over on the side of the rutted road inside the gate, and Ethan positioned the Honda for a quick return to the highway.

Whap. Whap. The Hummer's two front doors slapped shut.

"Good thing I'm not alone." Bella took the camera out of its case and presented it to him like a newborn baby. "Remember to hold steady and keep rolling. Don't shut it off unless we're getting back in the car. I'll keep them talking, so they'll forget about you."

Ethan glanced toward the gate at the sound of

somebody rattling chains. The way the creeps were crawling up his back, they might have been jerking on his. The smaller of the two gatekeepers emerged first, while the other one took care of the chain, lock and gate. Neither one was in a hurry to welcome anybody.

"What do you want me to do if it gets weird?" Ethan asked quietly as they got out of the car.

"Keep rolling."

The face of the younger man working the gate was partially obscured by a sweatshirt hood. The smaller guy—billiard-ball bald and bearded—strolled ahead two paces as though he was in charge. Ethan stepped back and turned the camera on.

"Mr. Mosher is unavailable," the bald guy said.

"*Mrs*. Mosher booked the appointment," Bella said, her tone friendly. "She said she welcomes the opportunity to show off her dogs."

The droopy hood shielded the younger man's eyes, and his lips barely moved. "Mr. Mosher likes his privacy, and he has the final word."

"Which is *no trespassing*. And no—" Baldy's hands shot out and snatched the camera "—pictures."

"Give that back!" Bella shouted.

Hoodie grabbed for Bella, but Ethan shoved him to the ground before he could get a firm hold on her. She staggered, caught her balance and went for the camera again. Baldy threw it down on the blacktop and raised a booted foot over it.

"No!" she screamed.

"Bella, leave it!" Ethan shouted. Hoodie was trying to get up. Ethan was forced to give him a swift kick in the ass before he could prevent Baldy from booting the camera. "Stay down or I'll break something," Ethan warned.

"You and me both." Big words spoken in a wary tone as the older man glanced at his prone partner and took a step back from the camera, giving the lie to his own statement. He pointed his finger at Bella. "No pictures."

"Elaine Mosher agreed to an interview with KOZY," she repeated with commendable calm.

"Well, her husband musta disagreed," Baldy said. "He's trying to make a living here, and you news people just wanna make trouble. That's what you do."

Ethan stood between Bella and the two flunkies. "Where's your phone, Bella?"

"In the car."

"Get in the car," he told her gently.

"That camera's checked out to me, and I'm not going anywhere—" trusting Ethan's upper hand, she leaned over to pick it up "—without it."

"You'd better hand it over, or I'll have to take it," the bald man said.

Ethan laughed. "You and what army?"

Baldy glanced at Hoodie, who was picking himself up off the ground. "You're the one threw it down," Hoodie muttered. "It's busted anyway."

"Get in the car, Bella."

"We gotta get the camera," Baldy said. But he didn't move, and Hoodie's hesitant step was unconvincing.

"Come on, punk." Ethan offered a cold smile. "Try me again."

Hoodie took a moment to consider. He turned his eyes from Ethan's, glanced at the camera and rubbed his carbuncled jaw with an oily hand. "You didn't get nuthin', and that thing's busted anyway."

Baldy pointed to the cattle guard that stretched between the gateposts. "Cross this line and you're on private property."

"Is that a fact?" Ethan eyed each man in turn. "I don't see anything that's gonna stop me from taking the lady wherever she wants to go. Bella?"

"I'm done with this for now," Bella called out from the car.

"How 'bout you two?" Ethan asked. "You done?"

Baldy glared at Hoodie, who shrugged as he backed off. "We'll just tell him they didn't have one," Hoodie said. "Or tell him it's busted. That's the truth."

The two men turned and started walking back toward their mighty Hummer. "You're about to get more than a kick in the ass," the older one said.

Ethan returned to the car, smiling. "I got mine in first." He closed the door and glanced toward the camera. "Sorry. I didn't see that coming. You didn't tell me this was hazardous duty."

"I didn't know it would be hazardous."

He glanced at the camera she was cradling in her lap. "Is it busted?"

"I don't know. I turned it off, but now I'm afraid to turn it back on. I'll leave it to the techs."

Ethan had never been so glad to pull a car away from a driveway. If it had been just him, he would have stood his ground, no problem. But he was no brawler, and Bella was no brawler's broad. "You shouldn't be going out alone on something like this."

"It sounded like just another assignment." She tugged at a wisp of hair escaped from the clip at the back of her neck. "It wasn't supposed to be like this. We arranged for an interview. We were surprised they agreed, but that seemed like a clue that there wasn't anything going on. But I think there was." She turned in her seat. "I think we got something, Ethan."

"You need a bodyguard more than a cameraman."

"I'm sorry. I really didn't—"

"Hey, nothing to be sorry about except the camera, which was my fault. They ever send you out to that place again, give me a call." He chuckled. "Hell, who'da thought reporting the local news could be that much of a rush?"

"There's obviously a story there. The Boston affiliate might even send somebody out."

"Is that good? Would you get to stay on it?"

"We'll see." She lifted a shoulder. "Commercial dog breeding isn't regulated as strictly here as it is in, say, Massachusetts. But cruelty is cruelty."

"They're not gonna blame you for the camera, are they?"

"I hope we got some pictures. If we did…" She studied the camera for a moment and then looked up. "Would you like to come over for supper tonight?"

"What, *you* owe *me* now?" He laughed. "If we got pictures, let's call it even."

"Okay," she said quietly.

"And start over. I gotta be somewhere at six, but after that, let me take you out for supper."

"You don't think I can cook?" She gave his shoulder a light jab. "Smart girls can't cook? Is that what you think?"

"Course not. Why would I…?"

"Is it true that smart girls can't dance?"

The line rang a bell right away, but he let her wait a moment for his guilty glance. "That's no way to ask a girl to dance," she chided with a smile.

He lifted his shoulder. "Did you dance with me?"

"Should I walk away and let him wonder, or dance with him and remove all doubt? Hmm." Squinting, she tapped her chin and then looked skyward. "Walk away, I told myself. Blow his mind. Nobody's ever done that to him before."

He smiled. "And?"

"I wasn't much of a dancer, was I? You would've remembered if I'd walked away."

"It was my turn to lead. I think that's what threw you off your game."

"I had no game," she admitted. "I was there because it was my cousin's birthday, and that was the only reason my mother agreed to let me go. That and the chance to take a picture of me in a dress."

"It was blue, wasn't it? The material felt real soft, but underneath you felt like you'd taken a bath in starch."

"Guess I was scared stiff."

He glanced, grinned, and they groaned in unison.

"Not anymore, though," she said gleefully. "Stood up to those two thugs today. Got the camera back. Asked you over for supper. I'm not even afraid of being turned down."

"I can be there by seven-thirty."

"Two-twelve."

"Can't stay that late. I'm a workin' man."

"*Apartment* two-twelve."

He grinned. "Just sayin'."

He was also a student. Ethan had done well in the correspondence courses he'd been allowed to take before his release from prison, and he'd been able to transfer a few of his credits toward a college degree, but now he sat uneasily in the back row of his first real class in nearly ten years. He wasn't the oldest guy in the group, and he sure as hell wasn't the dimmest bulb in the string. When they'd gone around the room introducing themselves, he'd simply given his name, mentioned his job, said he was training a mustang in his spare time. Nobody had asked him where he'd been for the past two years. He wasn't sure what his problem was, but he was uneasy with feeling uneasy. Come hell or high water, he could save himself as long as he took it easy. He was far from feeling any heat in this class, far from being in over his head.

So what was his problem?

If he was back to square one, if he was nothing unless he was easy, then where was he? *Who* was he?

That's what you're here to learn, Wolf Track.

It was going to be an interesting class. He'd tested out of all the bonehead stuff, so he was able to take a course that counted for something. An American lit class was a good bet for a guy who'd spent two years reading books like a fiend. He'd gotten the reading list ahead of time, and he'd already read everything on it, then started in on the list again. Take nothing for granted this time around, he told himself, even though his parole officer's advice was to take it easy, easy does it, *go easy on yourself.*

Hell, he'd never had any trouble going easy. Easy was no challenge at all.

It was time to try something different.

"Yeah, this is my second time with this one," he

said in answer to the teacher's question about the assignment at the top of the list. "But I'm noticing some things I didn't see the first time."

"Something sure smells good."

It was the right thing to say when a guy walked into the apartment of a woman who'd just cooked supper for him, but it was also true. He wanted to tell her how pretty she looked with her sleek black hair falling loose behind her shoulders, but he decided to play it safe.

He handed her a bottle in a brown paper sack and grinned when she pulled it up by the neck. "I almost went for the box, but then it takes a while if you like it cold."

She read the label. "Pre-sweetened, and with lemon. Excellent choice."

"The clerk said it was the best they had."

They shared a polite laugh. He glanced from window to window—the big one with the sofa in front, the smaller one over the table with the white cloth, two plates, one candle—and back to Bella, who was watching him, waiting for something. Not a kiss, that wasn't it. "You've fixed your place up real nice. It makes you feel good when you walk in."

"Thank you. It's California thrift shop. I love color, and I want to be comfortable."

Colors. Right. He took another look. "Earth, water and sky. You brought it all inside."

She smiled. "I hope you like chicken."

"I'm lovin' this one already."

She gave a sweeping gesture toward the table. "Sit down. It's all ready. I'll fix the tea."

"Can I help with—"

"I want you to sit." She disappeared around the corner of a partition, but she kept talking. "I was just going to have water, so this is perfect."

Ethan sat down at the pretty little table and listened to the sound of cupboard doors gently opening and closing, kitchen tools softly clinking. Home kitchen sounds, not institutional. It sounded almost musical. He wanted to be part of it. If he hadn't quit smoking he would at least have been able to light the candle.

"Guess what?" she said as she set glasses of tea on the table. "No, I won't tell you. I'll let you see for yourself later." And she was gone again.

She returned with serving dishes, one steaming, one piled with chunks of crusty bread. He was salivating.

"I hope you like cacciatore."

"Is that chicken?"

"With vegetables and sauce. Do you like sauce?"

He was ready to jump into the dish. "I'm a sauce fanatic."

She turned on her bare heel. "I forgot the—"

He caught her hand. "We're gonna ride double in this chair if you don't sit down pretty soon."

She gave him a funny look, and then she laughed, lowering her shoulders by several inches. "Matches. They're right over here."

He let her go, but he held out his hand when she came back. She laid the matches in his palm, her fingertips lingering, inviting him to curl his around them briefly, just to say thanks.

He lit the candle, and she served him his supper, candlelight dancing in her eyes. The food tasted so good he didn't want to talk. She looked so good smiling back at him across the table that he didn't want to eat. He wanted to look and taste and smell, and just be right where he was with this woman sitting across from him.

"Where'd you learn to cook like this?" he asked when they had finished their food and she finally allowed him to follow her into her neat little kitchen. "Your mom?"

"She gave me the basics. Meat, roots, corn, season with salt and pepper. In California I discovered variety." She nodded toward the serving dish as he set it on the counter. "Sauces. Lots of fruits and vegetables. I had a roommate who showed me what to do with it all. He'd grown up with all that fresh produce. Who knew herbs and spices started out as little plants?"

"You had a guy for a roommate?"

"Two. Two girls and two guys." Bella rolled her eyes and laughed. "My mother hit the roof when she found out, but it was already a done deal. I wanted to live off campus my senior year, and rent is really crazy out there. I was carrying a full course load and waiting tables as many hours as I could get."

"Sounds like you learned how to party."

"Did you hear the part about full course load and waiting tables?" So pretty, the way she lifted one shoulder as she turned on the faucet. "It was worth it. I loved having a lot on my plate. I lapped it up."

"It shows. You've filled out nicely."

"Thank you." She slid the dinner plates under a growing mound of bubbles as she slid him a second-thought glance. "I think."

"That's what I mean. You were always thinking, but now you look pretty while you're doing it. No matter what you have to say, it's a real pleasure for me to listen."

She laughed. "Why, Ethan, that's the nicest thing you've ever said to me. Also the screwiest."

"That's what happens when I shoot straight. It sounds screwy." He reached for the serving dish. Not much left. "What should I do with this? Toss it?"

"Oh, no. That'll be soup." She took the dish and scooped the contents into a plastic bowl. "That's the Ladonna coming out in me. Don't let anything go to waste."

"You called your mother Ladonna?"

"Only when she wasn't around. Which—" she gave a tight smile "—she isn't."

"You miss her?"

"More all the time. Don't you?"

He held up his right hand and wiggled a crooked middle finger. "I broke this playing football. She helped the doctor set it. I coulda sworn she was the doctor and he was the assistant."

She nodded, gave him a funny look as though he'd said something wrong. Or screwy. But all she said was, "Doesn't look like they did a very good job."

"I took the splint off too soon. Didn't wanna miss another game."

"Were you able to play?"

"Hell, yeah. I can always play."

The smile she offered struck him as sympathetic. He was open to all kinds of feelings from her, but sympathy wasn't one of them. He'd done the damage all by himself.

"Actually, I meant do you miss *your* mom? You must've been pretty young when she left."

He looked down at his bent finger. It had angered him a time or two, that finger. Jumped out there and made him look stupid. Caused him some trouble he could have done without. "I was five when she married Logan. Seven when she left."

"Left? I thought… I guess I assumed she died."

"She was just gone one day. I don't know what happened to her after that. I hardly remember her."

"If you were seven, you must remember—"

"I was seven, and I hardly remember her. Nothing else to report. End of story." He backed up to the counter and braced his butt against it, bracing for more even though he'd said there wasn't any. So far he didn't mind the questions, partly because he didn't have many answers. And partly because this was Bella. He felt good about her, didn't mind admitting, "I guess I thought everyone knew she walked out on us."

"Let's see, if you were seven, I would've been four or five. Ladonna would've been finishing up her nurse's training. We would've been living in Grand Forks, North Dakota." She raised her brow. "Either the news didn't travel that far, or it didn't make an impression on me."

"Damn. All this time I was embarrassed for nothing." He smiled. "Been tryin' like hell not to let it show."

"And you succeeded."

"Until now." He folded his arms. "Tell you what, though, I had a fine dad."

"Have."

"Have," he acknowledged quietly.

"So, do you want to talk dads now? That's where I missed out."

Good, he thought. *Over to you.* "What happened to him?"

"Killed in a car wreck. It wasn't until I was in high school that I heard he was drunk, *and* he was with another woman. Ladonna never told me that part. I had to hear it from one of the other woman's relatives." Her eyes challenged his. *See? So?*

"Maybe it wasn't true."

"I was a baby when it happened." She reached for his arm. "Let's go sit in the living room. Show-and-tell time. What's in your wallet?" She smiled. "Do you have pictures?"

"Of what?"

"Family? Friends? We're swapping stories. Time to look at pictures." She directed him to the sofa while she rustled around with some stuff on a bookshelf. "I'll bet you haven't seen a school yearbook in a while."

"You win, darlin'. Man, this is a comfortable sofa." He looked up, smiling as she sat down with an armload of books. "California thrift shop?"

"Rapid City furniture store. My one big splurge."

"Good choice." He rubbed his hand over the butter-soft leather. A school yearbook landed on his knees. "Do me one solid. Don't quote me on that blog of yours, okay?" He grinned. "Unless I said something intelligent."

They turned pages and revisited faces, and his own warm feelings surprised him. No regrets. No desire for do-overs. They'd walked the same halls, shared some of the same friends, or relatives of friends. Each had memories the other enjoyed hearing about, because there were shared ties to a place they were beginning to enjoy being from. Sinte was part of them.

The scrapbook Bella pulled out afterward was more personal. Memories mixed in with pictures of people and places—a nice little history book. It was something he didn't have, something he'd never missed, never thought about. Saving bits of the past made no sense to him. He decided it was a female thing, and he suddenly realized his life hadn't included females in ways that might make sense to one of them.

He looked down at the picture of a little headstone sitting in the middle of the big prairie.

"We always took care of my father's grave on Memorial Day," Bella recalled. "Ladonna never said anything bad about him. Never said much about him at all unless I asked, and then it was always kind of vague, some little tidbit she plucked out of nowhere. Like she was saying, I don't have anything to say about that, but here's something you'll like."

She brightened. "He named me. My father named me Bella. I found out what it meant. Beautiful. That made me happy for a long time. And then I put it together with my mother's name, and it made me so mad that they were both dead, and I couldn't ask them whether it was an accident or some kind of comment or curse. Or maybe it's a joke." She gave him a perfunctory smile. "What do you think?"

"I think you lost me. Had me at *beautiful,* lost me at—"

Her eyes widened. "Belladonna? *Deadly poison?*"

"Oh, yeah. Interesting." He slid his hand over hers. "Anyone ever suggest you might have a tendency to *over*think?"

"No. No one ever has. But, then, these are things I've never told anyone else." She squinted a little, second-guessing him. "Are you suggesting…?"

"No." He surrendered, both hands up. Whatever it was, he wasn't. "Not at all. I'm just catchin' up here."

"You have to wonder, right? Your parents are gone, and they took so many answers with them. So you think about what you have from them, you turn it over in your mind, and you wonder what more they would have given if they'd had more time. Don't you?" She didn't seem to notice him shaking his head. "Like when I asked—you know, the way we all do—where babies come from, my mother said they come from the seed a man plants inside the woman he loves. I liked the sound of that. It took me quite a while to come up with the next question."

"How does he do that?"

"Why does she let him?" She turned her palms up, empty. He didn't dare drop any of the words that sprang to his mind. "I mean, why doesn't she just plant it herself?"

He offered a lopsided smile. "I'm gonna say *because it's man seed* was not her answer."

"You're right. It was not." Her smile was pretty indulgent. At least it was a smile. "She said the seed comes from the man a woman loves, and that love is like water and sunshine. It makes the baby grow. I liked the sound of that even better."

"It's beautiful."

"It doesn't sound screwy at all, does it? It's pure and simple, and it sounded like the straight, God's honest truth."

"Should've left it at that. I would've. I never asked." Ethan slid down and rested his head against the back of the sofa. "One day I got mad at Trace and called him a name that, you know, started with *mother,* and Logan heard me. He sat me down and told me that was about the worst thing you could call a man. Hell, I knew that. That was why I said it. But the look in Logan's eyes…"

He shook that sad look out of his head. "I never used that word again. Not around Logan. I don't remember exactly how old I was when he told me the facts, man-to-man. Simple, straightforward, but respectful, you know? It was good, coming from him."

"You father—*biological* father—he was Indian, too, wasn't he?"

"Yeah. We had different fathers, Trace and me. She said mine was Indian. Never knew his name, but there was a picture of the two of them. I don't know where he was from, though. I kinda look like him." He chuckled. "Good-lookin' dude."

"Absolutely." Bella closed her scrapbook. "I'm glad you were with me today."

"So am I. Does that kind of stuff happen often?"

"I've been told to go away. I've had the door slammed in my face. But, no, nothing like what happened today. But that wasn't the end of the story. Did you catch me at six?"

"On TV?" He shook his head. "I was in…"

"That's right, you had to be somewhere." She glanced at the clock. "But it's just turning ten. You got pictures, Ethan. One full face and one sort of." She held her hand up to her eyebrows, shading her eyes. "But the really good part…well, you'll see for yourself," she promised as she reached for one of the remotes on the side table.

Within moments there she was on the screen, but the anchor, she said, was just teasing her story. "It'll be on at the end of this segment. It's big enough that it'll keep people in suspense for five minutes."

"You gotta be careful about going out to places like that. You know how to defend yourself?"

She lifted one shoulder as she set the remote aside. "I really do own a gun."

"You don't carry it."

"But I know how to use it." Another one of those token smiles. "And I know a few moves."

"Show me."

"Not unless I have to."

"Good move to start with. Keep your weapon a secret." He leaned closer and lowered his voice. "Wait until I make a move."

"I thought we were friends. I don't have to defend myself against friends."

"Expect the unexpected, even from friends." He took her shoulders in his hands. "A word is the only defense you'll need."

Her soft smile was a welcome sign. Her hand in his hair was a sweet surprise, its pressure drawing his head down for a meeting of smiles, mingling of breath, mixing of impressions made by moving lips and fingertips. He'd been saving this kiss for a long time, guarding it, fearing for it, thinking long and hard about the look and the mind and the heart of the woman who could take it from him. *Expect the unexpected* sounded good, but he hadn't expected Bella. He couldn't have known how good he would feel giving her an experience that had all the magic of a first kiss. He wanted to draw her closer, but he was afraid he would scare her away. Let her invite him, and let him go easy.

She lifted her arms around his neck, and he turned his head to one side, lightly taking the measure of her lush lips with his, touching and tasting, catching her breath in his mouth, tickling her mouth with his tongue. And when he felt her tremble under his hands, he drew her to him and kissed her thoroughly.

She kissed him back. She'd dreamed of this kiss long ago, made it happen a hundred ways, cooked up a thousand dreamy details—some raw, some over-done—and she'd been a believer for the very long time it had taken to become a woman. She'd held out for the hundred ways and the thousand details, and here was the first, the way of the kiss. It made her breath falter and her insides flutter. It made her reach up and lean forward, part her lips and greet his tongue. It made her a believer again.

And then, when the greeting was complete, she kept her eyes closed and licked the taste of it from her lips. "I haven't been…"

"Neither have I." He kissed her again, briefly. "Take it slow?"

"Yes," she said without thinking, and then on the other hand, "No." And that sounded almost as ridiculous as what came next. "Surprise me."

"I thought I was."

"Not yet." She'd dreamed a hundred ways times a thousand details. It would take…

He shook his head slowly, his gaze affixed to hers, and she had no idea what he was thinking as he looked at her, his hands gently kneading her shoulders. His lips came down on hers softly again, and then came the turn of his head, the touch of his tongue, the warmth of his breath and finally more kiss, good kiss, much more kiss. She opened herself up to him and welcomed the taste and the scent and the feel of him.

Then he backed off, giving her a little breathing

room, thinking space. She glanced up at the clock, and broke both the kiss and the mood as she sat up straight. "Oh, no, I think we missed it!" she exclaimed, turning to the TV.

He blinked. *Damn. Who the hell cared about…?*

"No, we didn't. Here it comes."

What she was saying didn't make as much of an impression on him as the sound of her voice, the way she held her shoulders, moved her hand. Oh, he got the gist of the report. He'd been on the inside getting the scoop firsthand. Anybody could see what was going down, and hey, he *did* get a little footage. But Bella looked terrific. The two thugs looked terrible. The camera mike picked up the few words that were exchanged before the picture did a three-sixty and went to black.

"Hot damn." Ethan slapped his knee. "My first—"

"Shh, here comes the good part."

Her rich, smooth television voice was truly the good part. It was familiar but different. Even more authoritative than usual. The raid that had taken place soon after her producer called the sheriff department was good, too, but Ethan was enchanted by the sound of her voice, the way it gave weight to the words and import to the story.

"It was a puppy mill," she told him. "I don't know why the woman said we could go out there and talk to her husband. She'll probably get in more trouble with him than with the law. The sheriff was able to get a warrant and get past the gate before they could cover up all the—" She pointed to Baldy and Hoodie walking across the screen in handcuffs. "Look. Serves them right. I guess those two tried to resist. The Moshers went quietly and made bail, but the two flunkies are still guests of the county."

"Who took these pictures? They didn't send you back out there, did they?"

"No, just John Carney, the cameraman."

"The real cameraman?"

"You're the real cameraman on this one, Ethan. You got the goods."

"I was about to, but then the news came on." They exchanged warm smiles. "That's really something, Bella. You uncovered a puppy mill. Where they… manufacture a lot of puppies?"

"It's like factory farming for dogs. We're running a follow-up tomorrow with a warning that it gets graphic. People from out of state answer ads for puppies, they don't realize what they're—"

"You and John?"

She frowned. "Me and John?"

"Doing the follow-up."

She smiled. Was he jealous? "I wanted to take you, but I really wasn't supposed to let you run the camera."

"What were you supposed to do?"

"I was supposed to get an interview. I would have asked my questions from behind the camera. Budgets are tight in the news business these days. But, Ethan, this was too good. This is really going to make a difference, at least for those poor dogs. They've all been rescued by the Humane Society."

He touched her arm. "You could've gotten hurt. You shouldn't be going out on stories like that alone."

"Hey." She laid her hand over his. "It's almost never like that. It's not a dangerous job. Taming a wild horse, that's a dangerous job."

"What's in the follow-up?"

"They got some pictures of lots of skinny animals crowded into cages stacked in filthy, crumbling shacks. And that isn't the half of it, Ethan. Yes, those bitches are used as puppy factories. It'll have to be edited, but people will get the idea. And I'll be interviewing the sheriff and maybe talking with the affiliate that put us on to the story." She was glowing. "It's my story. And I probably wouldn't've gotten any video if you hadn't been there."

"You could've gotten hurt."

"Okay, I could've gotten hurt." She squeezed his hand. "But I didn't."

He leaned in for a kiss, prefaced with a whispered, "I'm glad."

Chapter Five

Ethan's kisses took Bella out of her head. Her whole being rushed to be where he touched her, and there were no loose ends. His kiss went on forever, and his mouth made hers sing without sound. His hand tucked under her shirt made her skin tingle from the middle of her back to her bare toes. All she had to do was feel the all-over excitement. It didn't matter whether he felt it, too. He did—she could feel it where their bellies met—but that was just part of the process. She didn't have to figure anything out or plan the next step. This was happening. She was unfolding, stretching out and connecting up, and it felt right. Where one kiss ended another began.

Until it didn't.

Get 2 Books FREE!

Harlequin® Books,
publisher of women's fiction,
presents

GET 2 BOOKS

We'd like to send you two *Harlequin® Special Edition* novels absolutely free. Accepting them puts you under no obligation to purchase any more books.

HOW TO GET YOUR
2 FREE BOOKS AND 2 FREE GIFTS

1. Return the reply card today, and we'll send you two *Harlequin Special Edition* novels, absolutely free! We'll even pay the postage!

2. Accepting free books places you under no obligation to buy anything, ever. Whatever you decide, the free books and gifts are yours to keep, free!

3. We hope that after receiving your free books you'll want to remain a subscriber, but the choice is yours—to continue or cancel, any time at all!

EXTRA BONUS

You'll also get two free mystery gifts!
(worth about $10)

FREE!

**Return this card today to get
2 FREE BOOKS and 2 FREE GIFTS!**

 Harlequin®

SPECIAL EDITION

YES! Please send me 2 FREE *Harlequin*® *Special Edition*
novels, and 2 FREE mystery gifts as well. I understand
I am under no obligation to purchase anything, as
explained on the back of this insert.

235/335 HDL FMKU

Please Print

FIRST NAME	LAST NAME

ADDRESS

APT.#	CITY

STATE/PROV.	ZIP/POSTAL CODE

Visit us at:
www.ReaderService.com

◄ **DETACH AND MAIL CARD TODAY!** ►

If offer card is missing, write to: The Reader Service, P.O. Box 1867, Buffalo, NY 14240-1867 or visit www.ReaderService.com

BUSINESS REPLY MAIL
FIRST-CLASS MAIL   PERMIT NO. 717   BUFFALO, NY

POSTAGE WILL BE PAID BY ADDRESSEE

THE READER SERVICE
PO BOX 1867
BUFFALO NY 14240-9952

NO POSTAGE
NECESSARY
IF MAILED
IN THE
UNITED STATES

But he still held her and slid his fingertips lightly over her skin, and looked into her eyes like the besotted schoolboy he never was. She wondered how she looked to him. Like she would follow him anywhere? Because she would. No words required. All he had to do was lead the way.

He pushed a strand of hair back from her face and gave a reflective smile. "I can't stay tonight."

She bit back, *No one asked you to,* in favor of a matching smile. "It's okay."

"No, it isn't. You don't know me, Bella. And the thing is..." He withdrew his hand, pulled her shirt down in back as though he'd disturbed something on a shelf. "I'm ready to jump out of my skin right now, and that's not the way I want this to go."

"This what?"

"This...you and me. I didn't expect..."

"What didn't you expect? That I could give you—" she gave him a bold below-the-belt glance "—that?"

"Honey, I've been out of circulation long enough that even the slightest smell of a woman makes me so hard it hurts." He kissed her gently and touched his forehead to hers. "But that's not what I want. Not with you. Not tonight."

She kissed him back, a quick it's-fine-with-me kiss, and then freed herself. It really *was* fine.

"Can I ask you something?" she said quickly. Because asking questions was something she knew how to do. "The woman you went to jail for… Have you seen her since you got out?"

"Last time I saw her she was on the witness stand. Man, that was…" He gave a dry chuckle and shook his head. "And I didn't go to prison for her or because of her or anything like that. It was me. I was stupid."

"She said you drove off and left her after she told you to take her home and gave you the keys to her daddy's car." She glanced up at him. "That's what I read."

"She went off with somebody else and left me with the car." He leaned back and searched for the story on the ceiling. "We went to a party at somebody's cabin up in the hills. Craziest party I've ever been to, and that's just the part I remember. I didn't know anything about her father—didn't even know who he was—but it ended up that I had the car and not the girl whose daddy owned it. And the rest was my word against everyone else's."

"She's been in the news since. Her father's still trying to cover for her."

"She's a live wire, that woman. If you're lookin' for trouble, she can help you find it."

"Were you?"

"I was chasin' my tail back then." He reached for the straw hat he'd set on the side table, planted his elbows on his knees and toyed with the hat brim. "Tried playing football for South Dakota State, but they wanted me to take classes at the same time."

"Imagine that." Bella smiled even though he wasn't looking.

"Tried the army. I was fine with that for a while, but then I, um…" He shook his head. "Like I said, I'm not much of a hunter. Not with a gun, anyway. But, yeah, I was a lone wolf."

"Caught in a trap?"

"Nope." He glanced up, gave a self-effacing smile. "Paws on the ground, nose in the air, eyes wide open, nobody can touch this lobo. I got nobody to blame but myself."

"You sound like a totally rehabbed man."

He gave a nod and a wink. "One day at a time, kiddo."

"*Kiddo?*" She punched his arm. "I guess that explains why you can't stay."

"Hey, I don't call just anybody that." He laughed. "Okay, I don't call anybody that. I don't know where it came from."

"It goes nicely with that sexy wink."

"Now I'm totally deflated." He leaned over, took her chin in hand and kissed her, fast and firm. "I mean that, Bella. And this." He laid his hand on her cheek and kissed her again. Another kiss followed, and then another, each lingering a little longer than the last.

"Do you *want* to stay?" she whispered when he straightened, gradually separating himself from her.

"Absolutely." He clapped his hat on his head and

pushed off, hands on his knees. "I need to get back to Square One."

"There's something to be said for showing up where you're expected." She stood, too. This close, this enclosed, she was keenly aware of his height and his powerful build. Ordinarily she would have stepped back, required space. But with Ethan, this close was not close enough.

"And it's not that hard," he was saying.

"Who knew?" Silly comment. Overused filler. Bella wasn't fond of filler.

"You did. Some people have to learn these things the hard way." He took a piece of her hair between two fingers and let it slide through until his hand reached her shoulder. "Believe it or not, what's happening between us is new for me." Gently he squeezed her shoulder. "Like I picked up an egg, and something soft and sweet hatched in my hand. I don't know what it is, but I damn sure want the chance to find out."

"You didn't have a female judge, did you?" She smiled. "Of course not. A line like that would've gotten you off with time served."

He laughed. "Time to reel in my lines and hit the road." He took a step in that direction, and then had a second thought. "If I can get the day off, can I take you out on Saturday?"

"This Saturday?"

He nodded, his eyes bright with promise. "You like rodeo?"

Not particularly. "Is your brother riding?"

"Yeah, and it's been a while since I've seen him ride. He's doin' real good. Heard from him last week. He has a new girlfriend." He smiled. "Sounds pretty serious."

"The marrying kind of serious?"

"I wouldn't be surprised." He shoved his hands in the front pockets of his jeans. "So how 'bout it? You date real cowboys?"

"Not so far." She looked at him quizzically. "Funny. I never thought of you as a cowboy."

"How *did* you think of me?"

"I tried not to. You made no sense to me. Or *for* me. But look at you now. You've got the boots, the Wrangler jeans, the hat." She jerked her chin, pursed her lips in the general upward direction. "That hat looks as though it could tell some campfire stories."

Ethan snatched it off his head and turned it over in his hands, as though he hadn't seen it in a while. "Logan gave me this hat, long time ago. Thought of switching to outlaw black, but I'm pretty attached to this hat."

"I never thought of you as an outlaw, either." She folded her arms. "What time Saturday?"

"We'd have to leave before daylight, drive down to Nebraska. It's a midday show."

"If you can get time off."

"I'll get the time off if I get back on time tonight. Part of my retraining program." He tapped her arm with his hat. "You're keeping me in suspense here, woman. My ego ain't what it used to be. But I'll tell you what, I know how to get the most out of a twenty-four-hour pass. After the rodeo, I'll take you dancing."

"Oh, that's a real incentive. You know how long I've avoided dancing?" He cocked an eyebrow, and she nodded. "Yes. That long."

"The wait is finally over, baby. Wolf Track is back."

She laughed. "So much for a bruised ego."

It took a little over seven hours to get to the rodeo on Saturday. Seven short hours. The road was empty, the sun rose in a clear sky, and the conversation was packed with upbeat memories and down-home anecdotes. Bella had the local history, and Ethan's curiosity knew no bounds. She didn't mind letting him steer. It was his pickup after all. His party. He'd trusted her with enough truth to test her acceptance, and she'd passed. It was the kind of test a good reporter handled well. She was glad he wasn't in this thing—*what's happening between us,* he'd called it—for anything more than dinner and a show. No bed-and-breakfast. That was a good thing, and she owed him props for good sense. She really did.

They met Trace and his beautiful blonde lady

behind the stock pens when they got to the rodeo grounds. The first moments were all about the brothers, all backslapping and inside joking. No matter where the years had taken them, they were close at the roots. Bella and the blonde exchanged smiles as the camaraderie spilled over.

"You remember Bella Primeaux?" Ethan asked Trace.

Trace offered an eager handshake. "I remember Ladonna Primeaux. The nurse?"

"My mother. I take it you broke some bones."

"Nothing major. Got carried out of the Sinte rodeo arena once or twice as a kid."

"He's got a hard head," Ethan said.

"Runs in the family. But don't tell my—" Trace reached for the stunning beauty he'd brought with him "—special lady." He introduced Skyler Quinn, who asked Bella the inevitable question about having met before.

"You get Rapid City TV stations on the other side of the Hills?" Ethan asked. He turned to Bella. "Easy for me to keep a low profile around you. I'm just the guy with that TV reporter."

"I know what you mean. I'm the guy with the Dairy Princess." Trace laughed at Skyler for groaning. "It's true," he said. "It's a woman's world. Guys were put on earth to carry the water."

"Well, break out the canteen, honey. The special ladies need to rinse off all that soft soap." Skyler winked at Bella before turning to Ethan. "Trace tells me you're training a horse for the Mustang Sally competition."

"I am." Ethan adjusted his hat. "Hear you and Trace are entered up, too."

"Just Skyler," Trace said. "I'm the coach. The only horse I'm entered on is that little black." He gave an over-the-shoulder nod toward the pen at his back. Bella glanced politely toward the fence. "Tomcat, he's called. Good match for me. High roller. He can get a little snaky, but we'll rack up the points." Trace tapped Ethan's arm with a loose fist. "Your big brother's headed for the finals again. Mark your calendar."

"I won't miss it this time," Ethan said.

"Damn straight you won't." Trace reached *up* to plant his hand on his *little* brother's shoulder. "So, you like your job? Start your classes yet?"

"Yeah, I do and I did." Ethan clapped his hands and rubbed them together, clearly eager to move on. "Let's get something to eat."

"Nothing for me until after I ride." Trace turned to Skyler. "You hungry?"

"You know me. I can eat anytime," she said.

"Right." The two of them exchanged an intimate glance. Yes, he knew her. "But my little brother needs food now, and I think I know just the place."

Ethan stepped back. "You can just point us in the right direction. Then we'll meet you somewhere later."

"Not so fast," Skyler said as she reached for Bella's hand. "We've got some getting acquainted to do." She met Ethan's gaze. "And some catching up."

Ethan tipped his hat, offering Skyler a cowboy salute. "Thank you, ma'am."

"You've had a long drive," Skyler told him.

"Not quite as long as yours," he said. "Did you come down from Newcastle?"

"I live closer to Gilette," Skyler said. Wyoming was big territory, small town, which meant that mileage was not an issue. "Trace has been helping me out with the ranch, and I've been helping him ride like nobody's watching." She caught Trace's eye and smiled lovingly. "Except me."

"Why don't Bella and I go get something to eat while you two get a room?" Ethan teased.

"Mind your manners, kid." Trace gave Ethan a backhanded slap on the chest. "She's determined to keep me off crutches."

"Good luck with that, Skyler. My brother enjoys the agony of victory."

"It sounds as though you've both been to the nurse's office," Bella said.

"Emergency services only. The mark of a real cowboy," Ethan assured her.

Trace tapped his brother's arm. "Let's ride. I'm on a tight schedule here."

"I parked my pickup—"

"Way the hell on the other side of the arena. Come on, kids."

Trace loaded the foursome into his shiny white club cab pickup, drove a few blocks and pulled up in front of a restaurant called Better Than Your Mama's Spaghetti. He glanced at each of his passengers in turn. "What do you all think?"

Both women approved, Bella saying that her mother never made spaghetti and Skyler that her mother wouldn't let her eat it.

"Works for me," Ethan said.

"I know how to fill up that hollow leg of yours," Trace told him. "I've eaten here a few times. The spaghetti can't hold a candle to mine, but it's pretty damn good."

"Wait a minute," Skyler said. "Didn't you tell me you were a lousy cook?"

"I forgot to mention the three exceptions." Trace ticked them off, starting on his thumb. "Enhanced peanut butter sandwiches, everything-goes-into-it soup, and excellent spaghetti."

"He's right," Ethan said as he followed Bella out of the cramped backseat of the pickup and onto the sidewalk. "Trace perfected all three—when he wasn't keeping me in line. Logan's right-hand man. Riding herd on me was a two-man job."

"Two men and a bottomless pot of spaghetti," Trace said. "Took a little time to get Logan on board the spaghetti train. Devoted to his macaroni, that guy."

"That's the way he is. Loyal to the end and then some." Ethan shook his head. "Loyalty is good for filling graveyards." He glanced at his brother. "I think I read that somewhere."

"He's been there for you, Ethan."

Ethan nodded.

"And now he's found a woman who deserves his loyalty. Our mother—"

"I know all about our mother. Far as I'm concerned, a smart man doesn't put himself out there like that."

Bella took it all in. Trace was a rider; Ethan was a fighter. She wondered whether these were two more categories—*two kinds of people in this world,* Ladonna used to say—that deserved their own pages in her mental notebook. You found your niche at your first rodeo, and for the rest of your life you had it all figured out.

She slid quietly into a dark corner booth along the front wall, and Ethan slid in beside her. There were menus to be studied and water to be sipped, but the conversation was not over. Not until big brother said it was over.

"Cut Logan some slack," Trace instructed. "Every man gets one free pass on being a fool for love. Who was it that said 'Fool me once, shame on you. Fool me twice, you can't get fooled again'?"

"Somebody who got the quote wrong," Bella injected.

"Exactly." Trace cocked a finger and fired her a point. "But it's no shame to love somebody. Matter of fact, it's a shame if you don't. Maybe one quote doesn't fit all."

Ethan checked the front of the menu again. "Better than your mama's, huh?"

"She never knew what was good for her, little brother. You gotta pity her a little bit for her loss."

"I don't even like to think about her," Ethan said as he turned back to the list of entrées. "Why don't they turn a light on in here?"

Trace reached up and pulled the cord for the blinds, shedding considerable light. "I know what you mean."

He *thought* he did—Ethan would give his brother that much credit. And more. Hell, any credit to be had, Trace deserved it. He was a good man. He was Logan's true son in every way but DNA. If Trace didn't like to think about their mother, it was because of what she'd put him through, the hurt she'd put on him, the bad stuff Ethan didn't remember. Maybe he should be able to remember some of it, but he didn't. And the reason he didn't—he was just speculating here—was that he was like her, created in her image, *her* right-hand man. He shared in her faults. He—not Trace—was their mother's creature.

"So what's on the program?" Ethan asked. "Besides the next world-champion bareback rider."

"You talkin' to me?" Trace's De Niro was actually halfway credible. He drew a folded piece of paper from his breast pocket, set just below his sponsor's stitched-on logo, and tossed it on the table.

"Cowboy poker," Ethan announced as he scanned the program. "Thought they'd stopped doing that."

"You don't see it around here much. Hard to find takers after what happened down in San Angelo."

"What happened?" Skyler asked.

"What's cowboy poker?" was Bella's question.

"Some woman wasn't playing with a full deck, and she got her watermelon thumped," Trace said.

Bella and Skyler exchanged a look. "Colorful," Skyler said. "You mean she was—"

"I'm sorry, darlin'." Trace put his arm around her. "But there are some games women should not be playing."

"—pregnant?" Skyler's eyes widened.

"I picked the wrong fruit." Trace pulled her head to his shoulder. "Rest your worried melon right here, hon. No animals or unborn children were harmed. Some woman got kicked in the head was all." He turned to Bella. "They take four volunteers from the audience, sit them down at a card table in the middle of the arena, deal a hand and turn out one of the livelier bulls. Last player to leave his seat wins the pot.

Which is what tonight?" He nodded at the paper in Ethan's hand. "Five hundred bucks?"

"That's what it says."

"You're right," Skyler said. "That's not a game for women. We're way too smart."

"How about five hundred pairs of shoes?"

She lifted one shoulder. "That might be different."

"Have you checked out the night spots?" Ethan asked Trace. "Bella's dying to go dancing with me."

"The Killer Hayseeds are playing at a place near the arena. I hear they're pretty good."

Ethan grinned at Bella. "What do you think?"

"I think Killer Hayseeds sounds like the perfect follow-up to cowboy poker."

Ethan turned his grin on his brother. "We're in."

Skyler and Bella watched the Grand Entry from seats Trace had chosen for their view of the arena and the bucking chutes. His event came first, and he'd invited Ethan to help him set his rigging. Ethan seemed pleased, almost touched, or as close to touched as Bella had seen him. From her convenient perch she watched the activity behind the chutes, watched the two brothers confer over the equipment, and exchange words and handshakes with other cowboys.

The proceedings became nothing short of operating-room serious when Tomcat was loaded into the chute. Ethan took charge of setting the rigging and making sure his brother's glove was sufficiently rosined and his grip was solid. When Trace nodded for the gate to be opened, Ethan turned cheerleader. Bella half expected him to tumble into the empty bucking chute.

Trace did his fans proud. Tomcat rolled and pitched, twisted and turned, but Trace was unshakable. His score put him on top in the standings, and when he joined them in the stands, Skyler's kiss apparently put him on top of the world.

"Where's Ethan?" Bella asked.

Trace turned to look behind him, then turned back, frowning. "Snack bar, probably. Like I said, hollow leg. At least I don't have to buy his ice cream anymore." He grinned as he took his seat. "You got any chores you want done, Bella, you can pay him in spaghetti and ice cream."

"He helped me with a dangerous assignment the other day, and he didn't charge me anything."

"Oh, yeah, one other form of payment works." Trace draped his arm around Skyler's shoulders and settled in. "He can't resist an adrenaline rush. What kind of danger did you treat him to?"

"He got to hold the camera," she said, and then she related the puppy-mill story.

"Those two were lucky Ethan was in a generous…" Trace suddenly leaned forward and peered toward the far end of the arena. "What the hell?"

"What is it?" Skyler wanted to know.

"Little surprise in store," Trace said with a chuckle, and then he sat back and tugged at the front of his hat brim. "I sure hope these Killer Hayseeds turn out to be as good as they say. Sounds like something you might name a bull, huh? You like country music, Bella?"

"It's okay." She hadn't figured out what Trace was looking at, but she was working on it. Two rodeo clowns were pulling a cart loaded with a plastic patio table and four chairs into the arena. "Is it halftime already?" she wondered.

"Wrong sport," Trace said. "We don't go for a lot of downtime around here. This is what you call your—"

"Audience participation time," the announcer said. "Please welcome our four volunteer gamblers, in for a round of cowboy poker!"

It was Bella's turn to lean forward. "That's Ethan."

Trace drew a deep breath. "Yep."

"Is he helping with the... He's sitting down at the table."

"And that's the surprise."

"Not really," Skyler said. "He's your brother."

"You won't catch me messin' with bulls, darlin'."

"Has he done this before?" Bella asked.

"I doubt it."

A gate slammed, and a couple of levers clanked in the chute area below. Bella looked down and saw white horns, chocolate hide, no daylight on either side of the animal crammed into the chute. It moved, and the whole enclosure rattled.

She eyed the arena. The clowns in their droopy overalls and red suspenders were setting up the table for the four players. A moment later Ethan started dealing cards.

"The last man to remain seated wins the pot," the announcer said. "Five hundred dollars, winner take all. You ready for Ace High, boys?"

One of the men waved.

"I hope your hard head runs in the family," Skyler said.

The gate opened, the bull stepped out, and the game was on.

"This is crazy," Bella said quietly.

"I'm getting used to it," Skyler said.

The bull seemed to have eyes only for the smaller of the two clowns, who was jumping up and down like a string puppet. "Every bull wants a piece of Jackson," Trace said. "He's the best in the business."

The big brown bull lowered his head and shoveled the bullfighter clown out of the way.

"But so is Ace High."

"He's a bull," Bella said without taking her eyes off the action. "Bulls don't do business."

With a quick about-face, Ace High took a run at the closest player's hand. Cards flew, two chairs went down, and two cowboys scrambled in two directions.

Trace laughed. Ethan was still sitting there within spearing distance of a pair of horns, and his brother was laughing. "Forget the cards, bro. Save the jewels." He grinned at Skyler. "Hell, that's what I'd do."

On his next pass the bull took out the table, along with the third cowboy. Ethan was the last man seated. He stood to claim victory just as the big beast swung around, lowered his head and flew across the arena like a cannon ball, sweeping him ass over sawed-off horns.

Skyler and Bella shot out of their seats. The rodeo clown darted toward the bull as Ethan rolled out of its way and got to his feet. He gave his head a quick shake, recovered his hat and greeted the announcement that he'd won with a two-finger salute.

Trace laughed, slapped both his thighs and gave a victory whistle as he rose to his feet.

But then he shook his head and muttered, "Crazy kid," as he headed for the aisle. He turned and motioned to the women. "Let's go take inventory, see if he's all there."

"He's missing something upstairs," Bella said under her breath.

They met Ethan at the pay window. He'd already pocketed his winnings and was grinning to beat the band.

"Any blood?" Trace called out.

Ethan bent his arm and showed off a skinned elbow.

"Child's play." Trace turned a fake gut jab into a hearty handshake. "You coulda warned me, bro."

"And spoil my entrance?" Ethan shoved his hands into the pockets of his jeans, still grinning like a triumphant teenager. "Hey, remember when we entered the wild horse race at the Standing Rock Rodeo? This was like that. The kind of thing you do on the spur of the moment. You give it too much thought, you're gonna back out."

"You were about twelve, and I was—"

"Half as old as you are now, and what are you doing for a living?" Ethan tugged at his hat brim. "I rest my case, big brother. I know you won more than I did today, but I'm ridin' just as high as you are. Supper's on me."

"Supper? You just ate." Trace glanced at Bella as he slapped Ethan's gut with the back of his hand. "Can't fill him up, can't put any weight on him."

"I can wait a little while," Ethan said, all innocence. "Is there any dancing anywhere this time of day? Bella made me promise to dance with her."

"He's lying," Bella told Trace with a smile. "Dancing is the last thing I'd want him to promise me."

"What, then?" Ethan slipped his arm around her. "Make a wish, darlin'. I've got a pocketful of found money and I'm ready to spend it all on you."

Bella glanced at Skyler.

"Our first date I let Trace coax me onto a Ferris wheel. I'm afraid of heights." Skyler smiled. "Sometimes a little crazy doesn't hurt."

"I know where there's an old-fashioned jukebox," Trace said. "Take my mind off the final go-round."

The little hole-in-the-wall Trace took them to was enjoying some unusual late-afternoon business, thanks to the rodeo. Riders and fans mingled at the bar, traded change for tunes, and toasted winners and losers alike. Trace and Ethan made the most of the party atmosphere. They traded taunts and dance partners, told stories on each other and reveled in the rediscovery of each other's company. It couldn't last the way it once had, but that only made the minutes count more.

At least it did for Ethan. Not that he'd ever say anything that sappy, but he could tell that Trace knew. Trace always knew how Ethan felt, even if he didn't know exactly why. Didn't matter. They might be two very different people, but they were brothers.

And Ethan knew how Trace felt about Skyler. He was glad to see that lovesick look in his brother's eyes. Trace would make a great family man—hell, he'd looked after his younger brother like some papa grizzly—and if he'd chosen Skyler, he'd chosen well. He always chose well.

Ethan nodded as Trace flashed him a thumbs-up across the dance floor. He was a mind reader, that guy. He could always tell when Ethan's head was totally in the game. The message was clear. *You're doin' good, little brother.*

Ethan leaned back and smiled at the lovely woman in his arms. "Did your mama teach you to dance?"

"Obviously nobody did," Bella said. "And my partners generally excuse themselves after one dance."

"Guess your previous partners were mostly tenderfeet. Or maybe they expected to lead."

"They should've said so." She laughed. "Okay, yes, my mother taught me to dance. 'In case you ever have to,' she said. I also know how to get out of a headlock or a moving car *if I ever have to*."

"Relax and follow me." He drew her close and pressed his cheek against her sleek hair. "All I wanna do is hold you. I won't be giving you a score." He could feel the effort it took for her to relax, but she did. A wave of release fell slowly from her shoulders, and she was finally pliable. "There. Now we're dancing."

"We are?"

"We are."

She rested her cheek on his shoulder, and after a moment she whispered, "I like dancing."

It was a start. Ethan hated to cut it short, but now that he'd come back down to earth, he had to follow through with his plan. One day off was all he had, and he was not going to blow the trust he'd earned at Square One. He couldn't stay to watch his brother take the final round in his event, but Skyler exchanged cell phone numbers with Bella and promised to call no matter how things went.

Trace would do well. He always did.

"Why did you do that poker thing?" Bella asked Ethan after they'd been on the road awhile. He was surprised she'd waited this long. They were only a few miles from the state line.

And there was only one honest answer.

"For the hell of it."

"How many times do you get to be a fool for fun?"

"What do you mean? I came away with five hundred dollars. How does that make me a..." He glanced at her and chuckled. "Okay, but it was fun to watch, wasn't it?"

"It was not."

"I heard you yelling for me."

"I never yell."

"Ha. You called my name."

"The same way I called my dog's name when she was about to get hit by a car." She folded her arms. "The dog had sense enough to move."

"You have a dog?"

"I had one when I was a kid. She was smart about cars." She turned her face to the side window. "But men with guns, not so much. She was killed by a hunter."

Ethan felt a chill crawl down his back. "A hunter?"

"My uncle used to take her hunting. I'm the one

who should have had more sense. I shouldn't have let her go." She turned to him again. "Do you hunt?"

"Never have." He stared hard into the headlight path. "Never have."

"Three men in the house and you didn't turn out to be a hunter? What kind of an Indian are you, Ethan?"

"Wish I knew." Much better topic. "Hell, I don't much care who the guy was who, uh, planted the seed, but I wish I knew where he came from. You know, who his people are, whether they're hunters. Logan claimed me and gave me his name, but I can't claim his tribe. *Your* tribe." He flashed her a quick grin. "I want a tribe, hey."

"Hey." Bella smiled. "There's the Tribal rolls way and the Indian family way. You're in the family way."

He gave her an incredulous look, and they both laughed.

"Logan's been a good father, hasn't he?"

"The best."

"You and Logan have nothing but good to say about each other. It's none of my business, but I'll ask anyway."

"Because you're in the business of asking questions."

"Can't help myself, I guess." She cleared her throat. "Why are you keeping your distance?"

"It's not *my* distance, it's…" He lifted his shoulder. "Space. I guess."

"You've got it." She gestured toward the Welcome

sign as they flew past. "South Dakota has a good supply of space."

He let the hum of the pickup motor fill theirs. She was asking him a serious question, one he knew he'd created in Logan's mind. One that troubled his own.

"He was there during the trial," Ethan said quietly. "I couldn't look at him. I didn't want him to have to hear his name, the name he'd given me..."

It was a name that had fit him well. He never had to explain it the way Trace did. Ethan looked like a Wolf Track. The first time he'd written his name on a school paper, he felt like he was somebody. A boy with a man's name.

He'd wanted to do the name justice, but so far he'd come up short.

"It all seemed pretty unreal. I didn't take it too seriously. It was a party. A big steam-blowin' three-day bash. No one cared who anyone else was. I couldn't believe I'd be found guilty, couldn't believe I'd go to prison over something so crazy." He shook his head. "I didn't believe it until I heard those doors shut and lock behind me.

"And then Logan came to see me there. He never said anything one way or the other about what I'd done. He talked about anything but that. I couldn't let him keep coming to that place, getting locked down with me. I took him off my visitors list." He spared her a glance. "It was the least I could do, you know? Spare him that."

She nodded. "How did you cope with being locked away for so long?"

"I went home in my mind."

"But you haven't gone home since you got out. You haven't told Logan any of this, have you?"

He shook his head again. "I will. Soon." He gave her a lopsided smile. "Not that it's any of your business."

"I have a confession to make."

"Careful," he warned.

"No, I do. I've read everything I could find about your case. Police reports, court transcripts, newspaper reports. Anybody else's car, there's no way you would've spent two years behind bars."

"It wasn't about the car," he reminded her. "It was about the girl."

"Who came with the car."

"The car came with her."

"And they both belonged to Senator Garth, who's known for throwing his weight around."

"He's got plenty to throw." He reached for her hand. "Listen, Bella, it's over now. I came through okay. At least I think I'm okay. If you notice any screws loose, don't try to fix me yourself. Just walk away." He squeezed her hand. "Okay?"

"Walk away from what?"

"From trouble you don't need."

Chapter Six

He walked Bella upstairs to her apartment and waited without comment while she unlocked her door. But rather than turn to him, she pushed the door open and stepped inside.

From the scenes he'd watched and the pages he'd read, this wasn't the way your average, ordinary date was supposed to go.

He braced his forearm high on the door frame, just to show that he was cool right where he was. "How about a good-night kiss?"

She turned to him and gave him a not-for-prime-time look. "I'm not going anywhere. Are you?"

"It's after midnight." Which was prime time for

old habits, but he'd knocked himself out to get his date home at a reasonable time.

"You don't get a full day off?" She moved in on him now. "You might be a little reckless, but I don't see any loose screws. And if you have any, well…" She touched his chest with tellingly tentative fingertips. "Look at me, Ethan. I'm not walking away."

"This is your place. Tell me to go now, and I will." His arm came away from the door frame, but it would have been unfair to touch her before he had her answer in words. "If I stay, we're going to make love."

"I know." She reached for his hand, drew him inside and closed the door behind him. "That's the kind of kiss I want. The let's-get-it-on kind."

"That's not what I said."

He took her face in his hands and kissed her gently, the approach of an unassuming supplicant. She lifted her chin, granting more access. He took her in his arms, kissed her hungrily, the approach of a hopeful guest. She slid her arms around his back and stood on tiptoe so she could serve him fully with ample lips and searching tongue. He drew a deep breath, replete with her heady scent, and he took in the taste of her, the welcome-to-me comeback from her mouth.

It was almost too much for an appetizer, but not enough, not nearly enough, to meet his needs. He touched his forehead to hers, eyes closed, hopes high.

"I said we'd make love if I stayed. Will you do that with me?"

"You'll have to show me how," she whispered.

He lifted his head. "You're—"

"Not a virgin, no. I've had sex." No more whispering. "I've never made love. I don't *think* I have." Her smile seemed apologetic. "I hope I haven't."

"You'd know." He smiled. If he knew Bella, she'd done some reading, too. "For once, you won't have to think." He kissed her with absolute purpose. She wanted him, whatever having him would mean. And she couldn't help speculating.

He chuckled. "I know what you're doing, darlin'. I can hear it. Stop thinking."

She lifted her chin and smiled. "Make me."

He made her take him to her bed without further discussion. By the light from the hall he was able to get his bearings. The fat candle and the book of matches on her dresser beckoned. He struck a match, touched it to the blackened wick and blew out the match flame as the hall light went out.

Good. He wanted to feel her, to be felt by her, but he didn't want her to see too much. Not this time. He couldn't be sure what she would think if she put the feel of him together with the look of him in the light.

He turned and found her seated in a chair, struggling with one of her new boots. He took the heel in hand and stripped it off, followed by its mate. His own worn boots came off with an easy swipe of the hand. She stood quickly and unsnapped her jeans, as though she was afraid any dithering might bring on doubt. His doubt or hers, it didn't matter. He would banish it. He stepped in, took the bottom of her shirt in hand and peeled it over her head. Her hands were momentarily out of the picture, just the way he wanted them. For now.

He knelt before her, slid her zipper down slowly, tucked his hands into the open vee and spread the fabric wide. She wore a cotton bikini. He pressed his smile to her belly, and rubbed his lips back and forth over her soft skin. Her splayed fingers crept into his hair. He felt a slight trembling in her hands. He pushed jeans and bikini over her hips, and drew his hands down her legs. When he reached her ankles he lifted each one in turn, and she stepped out of her pants.

He skinned his shirt over his head, picked her straight up and stepped over to the bed. Then he kissed the top of each of her breasts, just because they were there, peeking over the cups of her bra.

He looked up. "You have condoms?"

"I said I've had sex. It's been quite a while, though, so…no."

"Yeah, me, too. But I have condoms." He let her slide along his body until they were face-to-face. "Hope they haven't expired."

Neither of them was in a laughing mood. He lowered her to the bed, and he hovered over her, kissing everything he could get his lips on without pouncing on her. He would go slow and take pleasure from giving her pleasure. He was almost certain he could do that. Take it slow. Give pleasure. Make love.

Her bra was fine and thin, perfect fabric for teasing nipples into tight beads while he rocked his hips against hers and coaxed her thighs apart. He took one nipple in his mouth and made the fine thin fabric wet, then pulled the strap over her shoulder, licked and suckled the tight bead until he could almost taste nourishment.

"Let me take it off," she pleaded, as though she'd outgrown the last bit of her clothing and it hurt to have it on.

He fully understood.

"Let me." He blew on her wet nipple as he reached under her and pinched the hook from the eye. She shivered.

"Is that good?"

She nodded.

He moved over her other nipple and treated it to the same mouth massaging and tongue lashing and pulling out of stops its twin had received. She called his name or, rather, moaned it, and the sound slithered into his ear and plunged straight for his groin. He propped himself on his elbows, used his hips to pry her thighs even farther apart and pressed his straining penis tight into the crevasse he'd created. Tight, but not too hard. Not too fast. No rush.

She thrust her hands into his jeans and grabbed his cowboy ass. Tough enough to break a knife blade, tender enough to bear the marks from her fingernails for days. Damn, it hurt so good.

"Take these off," she demanded.

"When I'm ready."

He slid down and kissed her midriff, farther down and kissed her belly, still farther and kissed the juncture of her thighs, and heard her breath catch and felt her suck everything in and hold every bit of herself at bay.

"I'm not ready," she whispered.

"Better than latex," he said, but he took her at her word and traced her slippery folds with a gentle finger as he moved over her. "Take my billfold out of my back pocket whenever you *are* ready." He nuzzled her neck and suckled her earlobe as he slipped his finger inside her. She gasped. "And then you can have my pants."

With his help she did what she was told, but he would not take his hand from her until she had come to the edge of wildness and given in. She started to shudder, and he would not let her stop, not without him deep inside, taking him deeper and making the wildness grow and scream and sing and burst open and pierce the dark with a shower of sparks.

She lay beside him quietly for long moments, enjoying the freedom to touch him anywhere she felt like it. And she felt like touching him everywhere. He was a beautiful man, and she took pleasure in his masculine physicality. She wasn't going to ask him whether the stories about prisoners beefing themselves up were true, but clearly he had taken care of his body. One day maybe he would tell her about the time he'd spent there, and maybe there would be some things she didn't want to hear. But she wanted to be the one he confided in. She wanted him to feel free, the way she felt free with him at this moment. Was that the effect of lovemaking? Trust and a sense of belonging?

No, she hadn't made love before. But now she had.

"Trace asked whether you'd started your classes," she said as she turned to him, knowing he was awake. He'd been touching her, too. "What kind of classes?"

"College classes. Right now I'm taking American lit and History of the American West. Thought I'd stick close to home this term."

She pushed up on her elbow and propped her head on her hand. "Are you just starting out?"

"Nope. I have a few credits in my jacket."

"Your jacket?"

"My record." He laid his hand on her shoulder and rubbed it back and forth. "I've got all kinds of records. My college record is the best one. I'm like you. Straight As."

"I didn't get straight As. I got some Bs." She rolled

to her back and grinned at the shadow the flickering candle threw on the ceiling. "Three."

He chuckled. "You set a pretty high bar."

"I did not. You did, with your straight As. I don't like contests. Never did."

"You don't like to lose."

"Who does?"

"Admit it. You liked it all over when I won that poker game."

"Don't be silly." She turned to him again. "Okay, I did. But mainly because the bull hadn't broken your body into a whole bunch of pitiful pieces." She laid her hand on his smooth chest. "I like your body just the way it is."

"Even with the ink?"

"It's growing on me." She dragged her hand over the contours of his chest, over his shoulder and down his arm to his tattoo. His birds must have been sensitive. Either that or they were actually mating in flight. She smiled. "You're growing on me."

"Yeah, I know. Try to ignore it and maybe it'll stop showing off."

"How long can you stay?"

"You mean time-wise?" She laughed, and he growled and nipped at her shoulder. "I could just eat you up. Are you hungry? I'm starving. Let me make you some breakfast."

"At four in the morning?"

"I've never met an Indian who was such a slave to the clock."

If he didn't want to stay in her bed, so be it. She threw her legs over the side and reached for the French terry robe she kept hanging over the footboard. "I thought you said you'd met my mother."

"La—"

"Shh." She turned quickly and pressed her fingers over his lips. "No names. This would not be a good time to wake her." Silly, she thought as she slipped into her robe. Her mother would be the first to say so. But she wasn't so sure. Sometimes she felt a familiar presence, and she wanted to do the unthinkable. She wanted to call it back rather than send it on.

"You need to brush up on your traditionalism, Wolf Track." She shook her head. "Slave to the clock."

"I said I'd do the cooking. I like to eat when I'm hungry." He gave a dry chuckle. "Whenever I can."

"Are you an eggs-and-bacon man, or do you—"

"Hey." He reached for her hand. "I'm a happy man right now. A very happy man. If I fell short, it's because I'm a little rusty. I promise to do better by you next time." He drew her hand to his lips and kissed her palm. "There's that word again." He touched the tip of his tongue to the center of her palm and made her shiver. "Time."

She didn't know what to say, so she put her arms around him and kept him there with her body instead of her words. She wanted to banish all doubt, but she wasn't sure what it would take. Words wouldn't cut it. He wasn't fearless, after all, and she might just be the only person in his world who knew it. It took him a moment to return her embrace, and she could only guess why. Maybe he was thinking too much, or remembering or yearning for something more. Maybe lingering in bed didn't appeal to him. Or maybe he was just hungry.

One thing was certain. There was nothing rusty about Ethan Wolf Track.

"You okay?" he whispered cautiously.

She nodded. She wanted a next time. She truly did. And getting all clingy might scare him away.

Keep it light, Bella.

"And I promise you…" She gave him an awkward parting pat on the arm as she slid away. "You're not short."

It was a relief to hear him laugh.

So she'd had sex, but she'd never made love. He was beginning to wonder if he ever had. He'd sure given it his best effort tonight. It wasn't even an effort. It was more like a gift that he meant to give, to feel it taken and kept, but it kept coming back to him. Maybe that was why they call it *coming,* he told his suddenly overactive mind. It was a rush, all right, but not the kind that rolled over you and blew away. The feeling was still with him, like a new kind of hangover. The good kind, which was something he'd never had before. Something nobody in his right mind would question.

But this woman was the queen of questions.

"What made you decide to try college again?" she asked as he poured the last of the pancake batter into two spreading dollops.

"I didn't actually try college the first time." The hot skillet started the batter bubbling almost instantly. Somewhere in the back of his mind a voice told him to wait until the whole face was full of blisters. Man's voice? Woman's voice? He shook his head. "I tried sports and parties and hangin' out."

"That's the way you got through high school."

"You notice every little detail, don't you?" He scooped up the first pancake and flipped it, golden side up. "About the time I realized it wasn't working for me anymore, along came a recruiter. I signed up. I figured Logan would approve of the army because he'd done his hitch and he never complained." He flipped the second pancake. "Not that I was looking for his approval—I wanted to go my own way—but I wanted his respect."

"I'm sure you had it."

"I don't know."

"Well, you have mine. Has he seen you flip pancakes?"

"He's the master flipper." He slid a fresh hotcake atop each stack on the plates in waiting. "I had one little problem with being a soldier." He handed her the two plates. "I wasn't very good at shooting at people," he said airily as he turned off the stove.

"Understandable. Is that why you don't hunt? You're not a good shot?"

He joined her at the table, where she'd already set glasses of orange juice and a platter of bacon. It was still dark outside. There was something cozy about sitting down at the breakfast table before daybreak with a woman wearing a soft white robe and a smile on her face.

Something that made it feel okay to let the stories just keep on coming.

"I shot *expert* with every weapon they gave me. That's the highest qualification you can get. They thought they had a real Sergeant York on their hands." He took a drink of juice and then gestured with the glass. "You know about Sergeant York. You shoot *expert* in history."

"World War I hero."

"I tore up those targets like a human paper shredder. They sent me over to the Middle East. Fine. I'm ready, willing and more than fit for duty." He tipped the glass and studied what was left of the orange juice. "Until the first time I had a real human being in my sights," he told her quietly without looking up. He wasn't gonna quit now. "Couldn't do it. I shot over his head." He drained the glass.

He cut into the pancakes with the side of his fork,

sopped up some syrup and shoveled the food into his mouth. It had no taste. He made a project of chewing and swallowing. When he looked up, she was waiting. No note taking, no disbelief in her eyes, no pity or judgment. She was listening.

He lifted one shoulder and tried to crack a smile.

"One time I put my weapon down and tackled a guy that needed shooting, sure as hell. I don't know why. Damn near got myself killed. Coulda gotten my whole unit blown to pieces. Went off the deep end, drinking, getting into fights. Ended up in psych. They sent me home with a general discharge." He glanced out the window. "Logan wanted me to appeal it, but I couldn't see it. Hell, stuff I did was flat out dishonorable. That's what they should have stamped on my papers."

"They must've given you some kind of treatment while you were in the psych unit," she said gently. Which was not really what he wanted. "Was there any reason why you couldn't…" He speared her with a look. *Say what you want to say.* "Other than the obvious? That the target is human."

"One doc said I wasn't crazy. Another one said I was. He didn't use the word, but that's what it boiled down to." He lifted one shoulder. "Pretty sure most of 'em thought I was fakin' it."

She didn't say anything, but she was looking at him pretty hard.

"If I was, I wasn't conscious of it. I wanted to shoot somebody. I really did."

She shook her head. "The only part that sounds crazy is you apologizing for not killing anyone."

"You can't run an army that way."

"You don't get VA benefits, then."

"I get medical. If I lose it again, they'll try to put me back together. But I don't get the GI Bill. You know, to pay for school." He poked at his pancakes. "I'd rather pay for it myself anyway. Let the real soldiers have the benefits."

"You'll earn yours like a real cowboy?"

He gave a lopsided smile. "Playing poker in the bullpen, yeah."

"Maybe with a little more psychiatric treatment you'd unlock some sort of—"

"Childhood trauma? No, thanks. Sleeping dogs, remember?"

"They're everywhere," she said as she reached for her orange juice. She hadn't eaten much. "We all go around stepping over our sleeping dogs."

"Which gives people like you some job security. You get to wake those dogs up and make 'em bark their fool heads off."

She smiled. "And free the puppies."

"Yeah. You do good work, Bella. You and Warrior Woman."

"How long have you been following my blog?"

"I wouldn't say I'm a follower. I don't get on the

computer that much anymore. I started taking classes when I was, um…you know, in prison. I got to use a computer. Warrior Woman did a whole series on Indian gaming. Another one on water rights. I used some of that in one of my courses."

"How did you figure out it was me?"

"I'd see you on the news." He took after his breakfast in earnest, now that the focus was on her. "A couple of words here, couple of words there, you put two and two together…"

"You were taking math?"

"I was taking Research and Writing, Miss Smarty-Pants. You helped me get another A."

"You're welcome." Her smile went with the smarty-pants. Which he knew for a fact she wasn't wearing. She finally cut into her pancakes. "Have you seen any of the posts I've been doing on the latest court cases concerning payments on Indian land?"

"That wasn't one of my topics."

"Senator Perry Garth is one of my topics."

"Ah, Senator Perry Garth." He wagged a slice of bacon at her. "The senator in particular is not one of my topics."

"Why not?" She snatched his bacon. "He's trying to hold up the transfer of public land leases from the Tutan Ranch to the Double D Wild Horse Sanctuary."

"I thought that was practically a done deal."

"Practically." She took a bite of bacon, gave it a couple of chews, and then wagged it back at him.

"Do you know what *practically* means in Department of the Interior terms? In Bureau of Indian Affair terms? If you get the right person pushing the buttons, you can slow a done deal down to an everlasting simmer. Just ask anybody on the Tribal Council."

"Never had much interest in politics, Tribal or otherwise. Like I said, not one of my topics."

"Water rights?" she recalled. "Tribal gaming?"

He shrugged. "Drinking and gambling."

She rolled her eyes. "Okay, what about the horses?"

"Now you're talkin'. Big Boy gets auctioned off, I want it to be part of something big. He's a hell of a horse."

"You're a hell of a trainer." She nodded at his empty plate. "Would you like more?" He flashed his palms in surrender, and she reached for his plate. "When are you going to show Big Boy off to Logan?"

"When we're ready."

"I want to be there. It's an important part of the story." She piled her nearly full plate on top of his empty one. "The Wild Horse Sanctuary story. There's so much to it, Ethan. Saving the horses is only the beginning. We're all related, you know. *Mitakuye Oyasin.*"

"Yeah, I've heard that somewhere. I believe it." He smiled as he took the last of the bacon. "We shouldn't be shooting each other."

"On that observation alone you should qualify for the GI Bill. What are you majoring in?"

"Staying out of trouble." He licked the bacon grease off his thumb. "I haven't gotten that far yet. I just started taking classes. It's gonna take some getting used to."

"History and literature. Interesting choices."

"I figured I'd better pick things that would hold my interest. You know, to start with. I've got people advising me on courses and job prospects. I'm learning how to take people's advice, or at least consider it. I've taken some swings and chalked up some strikes."

"You've had at least one unfair call against you."

"Best advice I've gotten lately is not to dwell on things. Hell, I was hanging over the edge looking for a better view. Guess I'm lucky I didn't fall any farther than I did."

"What would you *like* to do?" She tipped her head to one side and gave him what he'd come to call the counselor look. "If you had a clean slate, what would you choose?"

"If I had a clean slate, maybe I wouldn't have much to offer. Maybe I wouldn't know anything." She scowled, and he shook his head. "I'm not putting myself down, Bella. I learn the hard way." He grabbed his empty glass. Something to study. "I think I could teach. The kids at Square One, I can relate to them. They're like Big Boy. You can't push them, but you gain their trust, you can lead them."

"Pretty obvious, those boys would follow you anywhere."

"I'd want to lead them to trust their instincts. The good ones. Like you do."

"I've never heard of bad instincts, have you?"

"Good point." He laughed. "Can I borrow it?"

"You talk to Logan and you can have it." She reached for his hand. "Just call him. Your instincts will take over, and the two of you will get past whatever's keeping you apart." She smiled. "And then I can get a few pictures of you working together for my story."

"I don't have a problem calling him."

"Yes, you do. But you'll get over it."

"Is that what your instincts tell you?" He drew his hand away and started gathering up what was left on the table. "You don't know everything, woman. As smart as you are, you've got some holes in your education."

"One less as of this morning." His eyes met hers, and she smiled. "I've finally made love."

Chapter Seven

"All right, woman. I called him."

And this was the first time Ethan had actually called *her*, Bella realized. The very first.

"And?"

"And the party's at his place. Logan's a big believer in working horses in a round pen. You know, the sacred circle. I don't have one over here, so I said I'd haul Big Boy down to his place. You're going with us."

"Is that an invitation?"

"You want pictures, you'll have to take them this time. I can guarantee your safety. And Logan and me…all is forgiven. I guess."

"You guess?"

"I told him I wanted him to take a look at my horse, and he told me to bring him on over. That's how it's done. No hashing over who did what last year or last century. You just move on."

"Whatever it takes. I'm glad you're—"

"The deal is, he helps me come up with a routine that'll really show the horse off, and I help him paint my old bedroom. He's getting it ready for his next kid."

"When?"

"I don't know. Couple of months, I guess. That's a woman's question. Or a reporter's."

She laughed. "When are we going? That's my question."

"As soon as you can. I got to work on time last weekend, so I'm golden."

"You sure are."

Moving on had always been his way, but these days Ethan was taking it at a collected walk rather than a headlong gallop. He was getting used to the pace. He thought he would have to sign his life away in return for the use of Square One's horse trailer, but Shelly didn't even bat an eyelash. "You're in charge of the horses, and the trailer goes with them. It's your call, Ethan. As long as you bring Bella Primeaux back to visit soon."

His call. He had a call, and suddenly he wasn't averse to using it. He wasn't locked up anymore. Pick up the phone and talk. No justification necessary.

It had been too long since he'd seen Bella. Four long days. He could tell she'd been watching for him—she was out the door the instant he drove up in front of her building—and the sight of her made his heart skip a beat. Her black hair, caught up in a ponytail, gleamed in the sun. She was dressed in jeans and a sweatshirt—there was an autumn chill in the air this morning—and she carried the tools of her trade in a bag that hung from her shoulder.

She was always prepared, ever mindful of the way the bits and pieces of the world around her connected up. He admired her mindfulness. At the same time, he was fearful of it, and he wasn't sure why. Maybe she would see things in him he didn't want her to see, though he couldn't imagine what that would be. She'd read up some on his crime, and he'd told her the rest. She liked him anyway. She'd made love with him anyway.

She was something, this woman. As soon as she hopped into his pickup, he had to kiss her.

They talked a blue streak all the way to Sinte, and by the time they walked in the Wolf Track front door, Ethan was feeling just fine about seeing the man who'd raised him.

"I'm ready to paint," he announced as he shed his denim jacket and tossed it in the old brown chair near the front door where he'd always piled his stuff when he came inside.

"You want to do that first?" Logan asked. "Or hang up your jacket."

"Just testing." Ethan grinned. "You always said, get the chores done first, then you can play," he said as he reclaimed the jacket.

"That's exactly the kind of recall I need," Logan said as he offered Bella a handshake. "Glad you could come. Mary's getting out soon, and I want everything to look nice when she comes home." He turned to Ethan. "If you still remember anything I told you, it must be worth using again. Probably should write it down so I don't forget. I just got a pair of reading glasses. You believe that?"

"And you're having a kid?" Ethan laughed. He was feeling downright comfortable. "Better not be using pin-on diapers, old man."

"I wear bifocals," Bella said. She glanced at Ethan as they followed Logan and the smell of coffee. "You didn't notice, did you? I used to wear glasses. Now I wear contacts."

"*That's* what's changed. I knew there was something," Ethan teased.

"It has nothing to do with age." Bella assured Logan as he handed her a cup of coffee. "Neither does maturity."

"Living proof right here." Ethan took a cup from the cabinet and poured his own coffee. He was home. "What color are we going with? Pink or blue?"

"White. But I've already primed it, so it won't take too long. Hasn't been painted since you moved out."

"Sure hope the primer covered everything up."

"That's what it's for." Logan led the way down the hall, bypassing a row of boxes that hugged the wall. "Couple of boxes I've been saving for you and Trace. Stuff I thought you might want. Trophies, books, pictures."

"No pictures," Ethan said. He turned to Bella. "*No* pictures." God only knew what kind of pictures of him Logan could dig up.

"Too soon, huh?" Logan laughed. "Good thing we have a basement. I guess a baby will mean a lot of stuff we've never had around here. But don't worry. I won't be throwing anything else away. Only moving it to... Remember this one?" He plucked a book from the largest of the boxes and showed the cover to Ethan first, then Bella. *Where the Wild Things Are.* "One of his favorites. He used to know it by heart."

"I still do, so you can keep it for my little brother. Or sister. Wouldn't that be cool? A little sister." He tapped his father's chest with the back of his hand. "Hey, she's gonna look a lot more like me than she does Trace."

"If she's lucky she'll look just like her mother. Mary's beautiful. Hey, remember this?" Logan dropped the book into the box and turned his hand into a living puppet with forefinger and pinkie as ears, middle fingers tapping thumb to create a menacing muzzle. "Track Man's coming after you."

Thank God Track Man didn't complete the old routine by going for his armpit, Ethan thought.

"Look at him." He jerked his chin, pointing his lips the Indian way. "Track Man has a golden eye." His glance connected with Logan's. "I'm glad you got a ring this time. That's the way it should be. It should work both ways."

Track Man fell apart as Logan laid his hand on his son's shoulder—an earnest gesture—and then playfully pulled the brim of his hat down over his face. "You're about due for a new one of these, aren't you?"

"Nope. My dad gave me this one." Ethan adjusted the battered hat. "It goes everywhere with me."

"Well, put a drop cloth over it and let's get to painting."

Logan stirred the paint while Ethan showed Bella the view from his old bedroom window. The backyard was more than hobbyhorse land. It was Logan's real home. In the horse world, Logan Wolf Track was a well-respected name. He'd developed training methods based on Lakota tradition. He'd even written a book about them. His sons had learned what they'd been willing to learn. Ethan told Bella he wished he had paid more attention as he got older, but before he'd gotten "too big for my britches" he'd

followed Logan around the very pen they were looking at like a pup on the heels of its mama.

"Is too big for your britches anything like being
a smarty-pants?" Bella asked.

"Nope." He slid her a flirty wink. "It took me a
long time to grow into my paws, but the britches
were another story. For a while there I never did
have a pair that fit."

A few hours later, Bella stood on a rail on the
outside of the round pen while Logan leaned back
against the inside, a pile of horse gear at his feet.
They were watching Ethan work Big Boy on a lunge
line. Logan had expressed his approval of Ethan's
progress many times over with a simple nod. He reminded Bella of her mother. Sometimes a kid wanted
a few words. You might have learned not to expect
the effusiveness you saw in other parents, but you
still wanted to hear words. You wanted the people
around to hear those words.

They weren't kids, Bella reminded herself. As
Ethan said, they knew how to read sign. Their people exercised the kind of patience and subtlety that
mainstream society had forever misconstrued. She
and Ethan couldn't afford to do the same. They were
the bridge between two worlds.

"It's good to see him like this," Logan said. "It's
been a while since he's seemed comfortable in his
own skin. You must have something to do with that."

"I'll let you in on a little secret. I've had a crush on Ethan just about as far back as I can remember."

Logan glanced over his shoulder, smiling. "Probably not much of a secret, huh?"

"Oh, I think I kept it to myself pretty well." She laughed. "Or not. Thought I did at the time." She watched Ethan signal the horse for a lead change. She only recognized the maneuver because he had showed it to her earlier. "You know he didn't steal that car."

"'Course he didn't. But you try going up against a United States senator. Especially one who's been a senator as long as Garth has, and *especially* in this state."

Bella nodded, still gazing at Ethan. "Big fish in a small pond."

"You got that right. I tried to talk to his daughter after it was all over, see if she'd do the right thing, but it was no go. Garth got wind of it and threatened to charge me with harassment or some kind of..." He turned his head to her sharply. "Don't say anything to Ethan. I don't want him to know. I knew I was on shaky ground, but I had to try."

"Is Garth using that against you in any way? Politically, I mean."

Logan lifted one shoulder. "I don't have much to do with him politically. Have you started working on that story you mentioned?"

"I've been nosing around. I know the Double D

Wild Horse Sanctuary was granted the use of some public land that Tutan Ranch livestock has been grazing for years."

"Tutan's permits ran out," Logan said. "Sally got her application in, and with the leases the Tribe switched over to her and the backing of the BLM Wild Horse Management office, her case was ironclad. She gets the land."

"Done deal, right?" Bella shook her head. "Except Garth's committee's thrown it into bureaucratic limbo."

"Oh, jeez." Logan scowled. "That's not what I need to hear."

"As far as I can tell, it's the transfer of the public land he's trying to block right now. But can he interfere with Tribal leases?"

"He can cause delays. You know how that goes." He turned to watch his son. "You don't think it's because of Ethan?"

"I'm betting it's about your father-in-law," she said. "Dan Tutan."

"You think he wants to get at me? Because of Mary?"

"You guys all have this idea that it's personal. Sally thinks Tutan's afraid of her husband."

"Hank?" Logan shook his head. "Tutan liked to give Sally a hard time, but she doesn't take crap from anybody. She was standing up to Tutan before Hank came along."

"I'm sure she was," Bella allowed. "But in a pond as small as South Dakota, all the fish have a way of bumping into each other. You've got your brown trout, your big white lake trout, and then you've got your cutthroat trout." She shook her head. "That's a lot of competition."

Logan burst out laughing. "Ah, that is *beautiful*." Ethan was approaching with his quick buckskin as Logan called out, "You got yourself a live one, son."

Ethan grinned. "The horse or the woman?"

"Both." Logan offered his hand for the horse's inspection. "You ready to saddle him up? What are you using on him?"

"Hackamore, like you taught me."

Logan watched Ethan sort through the gear he'd left on the ground. Then he reached for an unusual-looking length of rope he'd draped over the fence rail. "I made something for you." He held it out for Ethan's inspection.

Ethan rubbed the intricately woven rope between his fingers. It was made of multicolored strands—shades of brown, gray to near black, tan to blond. Tiny ends sticking out all along its length made it looked prickly, but when Ethan shook it, it seemed to come alive.

"Snaky," he said appreciatively. "Feels like horse-hair."

"It's a mecate," Logan said. "It's a rein handmade from horsehair. Got my first one from an old vaquero

I met down in New Mexico one time. He taught me how to make them. It's all I use. You want try it out?"

"Sure."

Logan took Ethan's hackamore and started untying the old reins from the bosal, the chunky noseband that substituted for a bit. "There's something about the life in this thing. You can feel it in your hands. You get a connection with the horse you don't have with leather or hemp."

"How come you never showed me this?" Ethan asked when he held the newly attached reins in his hands.

"I'm pretty sure I did. Maybe you weren't watching." Ethan looked up, and Logan smiled. "Hey, I probably didn't say, *see this, Ethan?* I always figured you'd learn when you were ready. You've always had your own need-to-know agenda."

"I didn't realize how much I'd learned from you until…"

"You needed to know?"

"Yeah. Until I needed to know."

Ethan exchanged the halter and lunge line for the hackamore and saddle, all the while thinking about how easy it had been to work alongside Logan and Bella earlier, painting a room that held good memories and an innocence he'd all but forgotten about. There was only one wall he'd hated to run up against in that house, only one wall he couldn't quite paint over, even though its color wasn't quite clear, and he wasn't sure how much of it had ever existed outside his head. An array of pictures hung on it, and he couldn't quite make *them* out, either. He'd been pretty young when he'd moved into the house, but not so young that a normal kid wouldn't remember.

So, fine, he hadn't been a normal kid. He'd come to this town, this house, this life, with a whacked-out mother, and he had a vaguely bad memory of her. He didn't know why it had to bother him now. But it did. And now that the bothering had started, it would continue until he faced it and dug down to the bottom of what was eating at him. But for now he forced those thoughts away. He had a job to do, a job he loved more every day. His four-legged partner was learning to trust and teaching Ethan a lot about adjusting to change. One day at a time was the key.

It felt good to show Logan the progress he'd made. He didn't have to do much to put Big Boy through his paces, and the mecate made it even easier. He'd decided to show the horse off in reining, and for that he would gradually switch to a bit. But it wouldn't be the bit that would coax Big Boy to stop and spin and back up as though he were making dramatic moves of his own accord. It would be the rider's body, the shifting of his weight.

Ethan dismounted on the far side of the pen and looked enquiringly over at Logan, who took the hint to cross the ring and check on the fit of his gear. He asked about the fabric of the cinch, then offered the use of a saddle he thought would be a better fit for a short-backed horse.

They both knew the conversation was superficial, but Logan played along until Ethan hit him with the question that had been bouncing in his mind for the past twenty minutes, using his father's own term.

"I guess you had your own need-to-know agenda, at least where my mother was concerned."

Logan looked at him curiously.

Ethan stared at the house. "She'd been on her way out the door five minutes after she first walked in." He shrugged. "That's what Trace says. Seems like you should've seen it coming."

Logan smiled wistfully. "Your mother was an on-the-job learning experience. By the time she left, I knew she was gone for good."

"And that it was good she was gone?"

Logan closed his eyes and shook his head, still with that sad little smile. "I never said that."

"Maybe you should have."

"It was my need-to-know moment. I didn't think it was yours."

"I remember feeling relief that she was gone, and I knew I wasn't supposed to feel that way." Ethan ran his hand along Big Boy's warm neck. "Hell, she was my mother. But *I* knew, too. She couldn't come back."

"Why?"

"Because I didn't want her to. And I put her out of my mind for good. Can't even remember what she looks like." He looked to Logan for help with the shadowy pictures on the nonexistent wall. "It bothers me sometimes. Gives me a kind of a cold, sick feeling. Guilt, I guess."

"You have nothing to feel guilty about."

"I wanted you to…"

"Stop her? Get her back for you?" Logan laid his hand on Ethan's shoulder. "I'm sorry it went the way it did. If I could've—"

"No. That's not it." Frowning, Ethan shook his head. "I don't know what I wanted."

"Let's put it behind us." Logan gave Ethan's shoulder a parting pat. "How about we take a ride? I'll saddle up two more horses."

The suggestion was vaguely unsatisfying, but it was a relief at the same time. Ethan embraced the relief end of the spectrum.

"You got a kid horse?"

"I've got the mustang Mary and I decided not to enter in the competition because we didn't want to show you boys up." Logan nodded toward the side of the pen where Bella stood waiting. They started walking, Logan grinning broadly. "Just kidding. We're not putting Adobe up for auction. We adopted him."

Ethan smiled. "You're on a roll."

"And I've got that great little mare." Logan nodded toward the pasture.

"How about taking a ride with us?" Ethan said as they approached Bella. "Logan's got a horse for you."

She shook her head. "You two go ahead."

"We can double up on the mare."

"No, you guys go ride your wild mustangs. I have my own gadgets to play with. I've got some good pictures." She took a small camera from her amazing bag and showed him a couple of pictures of him riding Big Boy. "Want to see the video?" He laughed and shook his head. "I want to make some notes while it's all still fresh."

"In other words, you don't ride?" Logan asked.

Bella gave a diffident smile. "It shows, huh?"

Ethan put his arm around her shoulders, a gesture that, to his surprise, felt as natural as breathing, as comfortable as the smile on his face. "She does fine with a backseat cowboy along."

"Thanks, but you two go on," Bella said. "Just let me get a picture with both horses."

"We don't have to take them out right now," Ethan told her. He turned to Logan. "You got some time this week to maybe work with me on the maneuvers we talked about?"

Logan let the buckskin snuffle him up again before scratching the horse's neck. "He's got the deepest stop I've seen."

"Yeah, we've been working on that." And Logan's appreciation was sweet icing on the cake.

"His spin is coming along. A smooth rollback would be impressive." He nodded. "When can you get back this way?"

"You call it. I'll work it out."

"Why don't you leave him here and let me get to know him a little bit? Come back as soon as you can."

Ethan grinned. "I'll see about leaving the trailer, too. Then I'll *have to* come back."

Bella felt a little guilty about spoiling the plan to go riding. She would have been fine with staying back while the two men took off on their horses, but she was just as happy to head back home.

And surprised when Ethan took the wrong turn. They were headed down a dirt road instead of the highway.

"Aren't we going back to Rapid City?"

"Taking a little detour." He nodded toward the flat-topped, cone-shaped hill up ahead. "Haven't seen Sinte from the top of Badger Butte since the last time I rode up there with Trace. How long has it been for you?"

"Forever. Literally."

He gave an incredulous glance. "You've never climbed Badger Butte?"

"Never." She was probably the only person in

town over the age of ten who could say that, but that just made her special.

"I get to show you the view for the first time? You can see the whole valley from up there."

"Do you have to hang off the edge to see it?"

"Hang off...oh, yeah." He smiled. "No, that's just me. You can stand anywhere you want. It's a helluva sight. Can't wait to show it to you."

"I'm happy with an up-close-and-personal view from the valley floor."

But they were still bumping along the roller coaster of a South Dakota dirt road. Ethan didn't even slow down for washboards. He drove like every other male she'd ridden with on these country roads. She had done an accidental one-eighty on a washboard once, an experience that taught her to seek blacktop whenever possible.

"Did you tell Logan your news?"

"What news?"

"About going back to college."

"Oh, right." He shook his head. "Forgot."

"Oh. I thought when you were having that little huddle on the other side of the corral..." They hit a rut, and she quietly reached for the grab handle above the door. "Can't wait to hear what he has to say when you tell him."

"Why? So you can add that to your story?" He glanced at her. "I don't want to be part of any horse-turns-bad-boy-around fairy tale, okay?"

"I just meant…" She sighed. "Listen, I'm not climbing that hill, so why don't we just turn around?"

"It's gonna take five minutes."

"Never climbing to the top of Badger Butte for me is kind of like never going hunting for you. I can't deal with—"

"Look, Bella, I'm not afraid to hunt. I'm just not interested."

"I'm not afraid of heights. I'm just not a fan."

Ethan spared her a cold glare before slamming on the brake, spinning the pickup around and gunning the engine.

"Stop! If you don't stop, I'm jumping out." She pulled the handle just enough to make it click. He slowed the vehicle and pulled over, and she jumped out. And then he drove away. She watched him disappear over a rise in the rutted road.

What the hell was wrong with that man? She didn't like heights, okay? There were things he didn't like. There was no call to push—that was all she was saying. She wasn't trying to get him to take down a deer so she could eat meat. Not every man was a hunter.

And not every woman was a damn climber.

It wasn't a steep grade, but she was puffing as she approached the top. Like it or not, she was going to get a view from the high ground. She didn't like hiking. She certainly didn't like admitting she needed to start getting more exercise. But she didn't care about Ethan driving off and leaving her on foot. She'd asked for it. She'd *demanded* it. He'd said it himself—told her to walk away if he started acting like he had a few screws loose. She was a wise woman, a warrior woman, and she was doing just that. Walking away.

It was too bad she'd left her bag in the pickup.

The view from the top of the rise gave her a thrill. She could see herself bursting into song. She could also see herself heading down the other side and marching right past the pickup parked at the bottom and the man leaning against the driver's side door.

And she almost did.

"I'm sorry, Bella."

She stopped.

"Please ride with me."

She turned and gave him the coldest look in her arsenal—and she had some icy ones stored up.

"I didn't mean to scare you." He pushed away from the pickup, shoved his hands in his pockets and scraped his boot heel across the hardpan as he approached. "All right, I did, but I won't do it again. Ever."

Was that sincerity in those hooded eyes?

Damn, she should just keep walking.

But she didn't. She'd walked far enough. "I'm afraid of heights." She grabbed a handful of soft T-shirt and pressed her fist against hard belly. "Understand?"

"Perfectly."

"No pressure. No ifs, ands or buts. I don't do heights." She pulled back and punched this time. His gut was rock hard. "And no teasing. Got that?"

"Yes, ma'am." He was doing pretty well on the straight-face score.

She narrowed her eyes. "Because you don't want anybody trying to coax *your* monsters out from under your bed."

"You're right. That's why I don't own a bed."

"Wherever you sleep, then." She let go of his shirt. "You and Logan were having yourselves a real reunion, Ethan. You could've topped it off with your college news."

"It's no big deal." He lifted his gaze above her head and shrugged. "Because, it's not like I've graduated or anything. I'm just taking classes."

"And I read a script in front of a camera. Your father goes to meetings and listens to a rehash of the proposals that didn't get passed last month. Your brother hangs on to a bucking horse for ten seconds at a time."

"Eight seconds."

"Not *even* ten seconds at a time."

He looked her in the eyes again. The corners of his mouth started twitching, and he couldn't hold back. He had to laugh.

And she had to laugh with him.

He draped his arm around her shoulders, and she

took his hand with hers, lacing their fingers together. He walked her around the front of the pickup.

"You wouldn't really have jumped out of the pickup if I hadn't stopped, would you?"

"I'll never tell." She glanced up, offering a smug smile. "I might need that one again."

"You wanna hang out tonight?"

"I don't hang out."

"I do." He opened the pickup door. "Your place?"

"Where else?"

Their lovemaking, breathtakingly hot and spicy, was filled with the taste of salt and the pungent scent of musk. He took her standing, and she rode him sitting. They held each other off one more moment and pushed each other one more fraction of a fraction, and called each other's names one more way and one more time.

Their lovemaking was sweet and slow, filled with whispers and warm breath, and the fine feel of smooth skin and long cool hair and short damp curls. He took her gently and she received him deeply, and they traded endearments neither had ever spoken before. And when they were sated with all the pleasure either had ever imagined, they wrapped each other in their arms and legs and moved languidly to touch and reassure.

"Ethan."

"Hmm?"

"I admire you."

He gave a self-satisfied chuckle. "You've got a crush on me."

"That's old news." She traced a circle around his flat nipple. "I've learned a lot about you since you came to my rescue at the Hitching Post."

"The itching Post. Didn't you notice the sign? The *H* is missing. That leaves you *itching*."

"You, maybe." She offered a saucy smile. "What are you going to do about it?"

"Enjoy it. It's that kind of itch. The kind you don't wanna scratch off." He closed his eyes and smiled. There was much to be enjoyed. "What do you admire?"

She pressed her lips to his chest. "The way you handle yourself. You're your own man. I like being with you. I like being my own woman while I'm with you." She pressed her lips to his chest. "I'm glad you don't want to scratch me off, but if you have an itch, a little scratching might be in order."

He kissed her forehead. "I've made some big choices in my life that didn't work for me. I don't want you to find yourself thinking of me that way." He threaded his fingers through her hair. Here in the dark it was easy to talk. There was no heaviness. It was all wrung out of them, and so he could say without hesitation, "I don't wanna be the first bad choice you've ever made."

"You're a big choice for me, I'll grant you that.

And so far, so very good." She scooted up along his side and rested her chin on the kiss she'd imprinted on his skin as surely as the tattoo artist he'd visited long ago. "But you have a way of distracting me when I want to say something, especially when it's about you."

"The scratching thing? That's a pretty basic male instinct, Bella. Even if I do it better than anyone else you know, I'm still just another—"

"It's not a competition, Ethan. I admire *you*. You're not afraid to make more big choices just because you've run into some obstacles. You haven't let the detours break your stride." She slid her hand over his hip. "I love to watch you walk, by the way."

"Same here. You should've seen yourself marching down that hill."

She growled.

"Look, I know where you're goin' with this. I feel good about what I'm doing, but I'm building on a pretty fragile foundation. Let me work on it awhile. Okay?" He twirled her hair around his finger. It had life, like the mecate. "Your mom never got to see you on TV, did she?"

"No."

"She knew where you were headed, though. She knew who you were." She laid her cheek against him. "You're beautiful, Bella. You know that, don't you?" Her response—a small sound—wasn't quite an agreement. "She knew that, too. Hey, Belladonna is one of those miracle drugs, like aspirin. I looked it up. It's powerful. It helps people, but you don't wanna abuse it. Ladonna gave you her strength, and you ran with it."

"Logan's done the same for you."

"I ran the other way. But I'm back. Still, you're way ahead of me, Bella. I need time to catch up."

"The story behind the Wild Horse Sanctuary is something we can run with together. And there's more. I think there's a lot more."

"More story?"

"More *to* the story. More history."

"Is that your specialty? Digging up the past?"

"Let's see…what courses did you say *you* chose to start with?"

He groaned. "Damn, you're good."

Ethan woke up in a cold sweat. A bright horror filled his head and popped his eyes open, peeled them wide against the dark. He didn't know where he was, whether he was awake or dreaming. Part of him was in a dark place, and the rest was still somewhere else.

Somebody was dead out there in the field. He'd heard an explosion, but what flew wasn't shrapnel or body parts. It was a cloud of birds. Screeching birds, wildly flapping, desperately churning the air. A man popped up from the tall grass. And then *pop! Pop!* Firecrackers made Ethan jump and cover his ears, and the man's face went all red. And then he vanished.

Ethan rubbed his hand over his own face, hoping it was dry. It wasn't, but it didn't feel red. He knew what red felt like. Warm and watery at first, but when it went cold it felt sticky.

God help him, he was dreaming again. He'd gone months without landing in whacked-out places in his head at night, seeing things that looked like they'd been slapped together by a madman wielding a paint-brush—eyeballs popping out of birds' nests, Indians slithering through the grass like alligators, hand-cuffed men dressed in orange and women washing their hair in blood.

He wasn't going back for any more medical treat-ment. No more medication—all that did was make him groggy. He was gonna tough this thing out. It had almost faded away, and he could make that hap-pen again. Stay busy, stay healthy, wait the devil out.

He turned to the woman lying close to his side, and he kissed her hair. She hadn't stirred, so he must not have made any noise. He must not have thrashed around. He was taking a chance of exposing himself by staying the whole night. Exposing the nature of his…little disorder.

Hell, plenty of people had nightmares. They weren't all crazy, and neither was he. Hadn't Bella just pointed out to him all the progress he was making? And it wasn't like she didn't know where he'd been.

Sometimes he wondered if *he* knew where he'd been. There was something different about this night's dream, though. There was urgency to it, the sense of a presence just below the surface.

But the surface of what?

Chapter Eight

It had been almost a week since Bella had seen Ethan, and she wasn't expecting to run into him at the Double D. The sight of his pickup barreling down the gravel road gave her butterflies. Here she was, doing her job, and there *he* was, parking in front of the house, and she couldn't wait to stow away the tools of her trade and turn to trading wisecracks and secret smiles with her cowboy.

Her cowboy. It sounded crazy, even within the private walls of her suddenly giddy head.

But she wasn't starry-eyed enough to start shirking her responsibilities. Final preparations were being made for the Wild Horse Makeover Horse Show, and she was finishing up her background work. That was her pretext, anyway. She was covering the big finale, but she was also getting closer to pinning down Senator Perry Garth's involvement with the allocation of the land that belonged to her people.

She'd met with the treasurer of the Cheyenne people in Montana—one of the tribes that was fighting with the Interior Department over missing payments—and she was convinced that Senator Garth's fingerprints were all over those billion-dollar bills. She knew she was working both ends against the middle on this story—and the Double D was somewhere in the middle—but that was the way investigative reporting worked sometimes. You started with one small piece out of place—a small player, a local matter—and you searched for a hole left by that piece.

And if you cared about the piece, if you couldn't abide that hole, your passion for the search intensified. The competition finale was her KOZY assignment. She was working on the Garth connection independently, and there was something a little too cozy going on with the senator. Why would he interfere with a Bureau of Land Management recommendation, stand in opposition to a determination made by the Tribal Council and essentially expend valuable political clout for a relatively small-time rancher like Tutan? Just because Tutan offered a good place to go hunting?

Suddenly there was all manner of coziness.

And more than one stimulus for passion.

Ethan waited for her to reach him and kissed her when she did.

"You don't mind showing us off publicly?" she asked.

"I don't see any public around." He glanced left and right. "Do you?"

"Not at the moment."

"I keep forgetting, you really have a public."

"I'd like to forget it. Well, most days. But the closer I get to home, the less I have to worry about it."

"It's been a while since I made the news. I don't think anybody remembers."

"I'm not worried about that." She reached up and tugged on his hat brim. "Not at all. But when you win this contest, you'll be making the news again. Is that okay with you?"

"I ain't livin' in the past, darlin'." He took her hands in his. "The present suits me better every day."

"What are you up to today?"

He nodded toward the front door. "Checkin' in with Sally on the facilities for the horse show. Logan's been working with me on a routine that'll show Big Boy off to his best advantage. I want to make sure—"

"Well, I'll be damned."

They turned to find Sally Night Horse watching them through the screen door.

"No, you won't, Sally." The deep voice came from behind her. "I did two funeral solos last month. In my heart I was singing for your salvation." A tall handsome Indian appeared in the doorway behind Sally, who was pushing the door open. "If my wife's trying to make another match, you might wanna check the fine print. Make sure she's got you registered for heaven."

"Aren't they adorable, Hank? You've met Logan Wolf Track's boy, haven't you?"

Hank Night Horse met Ethan at the top of the porch steps with a handshake, and then he extended his hand to Bella. "You've been taking more pictures today?"

"Never enough pictures. Actually, I was hoping we could talk."

"You guys can talk," Hank said. "I'm just a quiet man trying to keep up with a force of nature." He put his arm around Sally's shoulders and leaned close to her ear. "This man is not a boy. And no man wants to be called *adorable*."

"I mean as a couple. I had nothing to do with this one, but I see no reason why the Double D can't take credit." Sally waved her visitors inside. "We've got our hands full right now with the sanctuary, but in my next life I'm running one of those online dating services. I think I could make a fortune."

She gestured toward the office door. "Come on in and have a seat. We're just discussing a little hiccup we might be holding our breath over while we get this horse show on the road here. Like we need another detail to worry about right now."

Hank sat back against a counter, arms folded, while Sally took a seat in the wheelchair that served as an office chair in good times and as legs when hers weren't getting her where she wanted to go.

Bella started for a folding chair, but Sally pointed to a daybed piled with pillows. "You two take the... we'll call it the love seat. Bella, remember how you offered to help us get some community support messages on TV? You know, about donating prizes for the competition?"

Bella nodded, but her smile was for Ethan as she patted the space beside her on the daybed.

"We don't need any more donations right now. Annie—my sister—she has a generous brother-in-law who's ponying up for all that. Says he needs the tax write-off. What we need is public support. We need horse lovers."

"The news coverage should help."

"And we've got Skyler Quinn—" she glanced at Ethan "—your brother's Skyler, another Double D matchup. We've got Skyler working on a documentary.

"But here's the latest thing that worries me." She snatched a folded paper off her desk and snapped it open. "I got a letter today about the public land. Some glitch in the paperwork. I've already fired off a response. I told them to ask their assistant. She's the one who knows where the mother of all glitches is buried."

"I'm pretty sure the holdup is a few pay grades higher than assistant," Bella said. "I have some low-level friends in high-level places. Reliable sources, we call them. Your neighbor, Mr. Tutan, doesn't want to give up the land. He has one of our South Dakota senators doing his bidding." She glanced at Ethan. "I know this hits close to home in more ways than one, but—"

"I got no skin in this game," Ethan told her. He looked at Sally. "Horsehide, but no skin."

Bella felt a chill. If she wasn't mistaken, Ethan's beautiful black eyes had just gone stone-cold.

"But the decision's been made." Sally looked up at her husband and then turned to Bella. "Hasn't it? What exactly do your reliable sources say?"

"It's being reviewed. What does the letter say the holdup is?"

Sally lifted one shoulder. "That they're waiting on some signatures."

"There's a big investigation going on with the Bureau of Indian Affairs," Bella said. "Billions of dollars in lease payments on Indian trust land are missing. Completely unaccounted for. Apparently there's been a slow, steady leak that's been going on for years."

"Stolen?" Sally asked.

"They don't know," Hank put in. "Some stolen, some never paid, they can't figure it out. Probably never will. It's just gone, and who has time to track it down? You know how that goes." He glanced at Bella. "Some of us do, anyway. Most of our Indian trust land has been handed down many times over, and Tribal members don't designate heirs, so it gets chopped up among the direct descendants. Since this has been going on for generations, you maybe get a statement showing pages of parcels of land that you have pennies' worth of interest in. The Bureau's a mess, which makes it easy to rob. You don't even have to bother to cover up your tracks. The red tape does it for you."

"That's terrible," Sally said.

Hank smiled. "Oh, yeah. It's terrible."

Bella chimed in. "Senator Garth has been sitting on relevant committees for as long as he's been in the senate—which is longer than most of us have been alive—and, of course, he says he's outraged. But there isn't much of a paper trail. There's an abundance of paper, but no trail. So he's all for offering a settlement, and then we let bygones be bygones."

"I don't see how our little public land lease would be connected."

"It probably isn't," Bella assured Sally. "Not directly. But according to my source, Garth is being questioned pretty closely. And on another front, he's suddenly particularly interested in certain parcels of public land, including Tutan's leases."

Sally frowned. "Why?"

"They're friends," Bella said. "They have been for years. According to my sources, Garth loves to hunt. He used to bring his pals out to Tutan's place every fall to go hunting. Tutan hosted quite a party back in the day. And Garth made sure Tutan had all the grazing permits and leases he could possibly want."

Hank was studying the toes of his boots. "Do you have any idea how far back this annual tradition goes?"

"Twenty years," Bella said. "Maybe more."

"My father used to work for Tutan." Hank looked up, his eyes suddenly haunted. "Seasonal laborer, but during hunting season a lotta times he'd stay on to help out with some of those parties. He disappeared. By the time they found his body..." He was talking to Bella's reporter persona now. "Well, they said he'd been drinking and he'd probably shot himself. Could've been an accident. Maybe suicide. Hard to tell, since he'd been dead for weeks."

"Was he with one of those hunting parties when he went missing?"

"The last time we heard from my father, he called to let us know he'd be staying down here for a couple more weeks, working for Tutan. But after he disappeared, Tutan said he thought my father had gone home to North Dakota after they brought the hay in.

Some coyote hunter actually stumbled over my dad's body. There was an investigation. Tutan said he'd had some hunters come through, but he couldn't be sure."

"Was there a gun?"

Bella turned to Ethan. His question surprised her. He'd been so quiet that the very sound of his voice surprised her. He was staring at his hands. "Did they find a gun with his body?"

"They found a shotgun that had been reported stolen and a decomposed body full of shot. My dad didn't own a gun. He didn't hunt. His job was bird-dogging. Flushing pheasants—"

"Out of the brush. They put the gun…" Ethan cleared his throat. Bella could feel him shaking. "They probably put the gun there."

"They?" Hank said.

Ethan shook his head blindly. "Whoever."

"How long ago did it happen?" Bella asked Hank.

"Twenty-one years."

Ethan turned to her. "Is this all part of your story?"

"It could be. Hank, how much—"

"I've gotta get going." Ethan patted Bella's knee and stood to leave. "This looks like another job for Warrior Woman."

"It's definitely…" Bella got to her feet. "Ethan, you wanted to ask about the final—"

"The show, yeah. Some of the details…" He didn't

even spare her a glance. "I'm working out my routine," he told Sally. "I'll call you."

And then Ethan was gone. She hadn't imagined his reaction to Hank's story. He was trembling. She wanted to tear after him, but if she caught up, the questions would roll off her tongue, and he didn't need that right now. She was dying for answers. He was running from the questions. What a pair.

"Bella," Hank said, "what's this all about? What story?"

"I'm not sure." She turned away from watching one of her passions retreat and faced the question that could be at the heart of the other. "I'd like to know more about your father's death."

"So would I."

She needed a corner piece of the puzzle so she could start framing the problem. "What was his name?"

"John Night Horse."

Ethan's dreams were built on pieces of memory. He knew that now. There was a trail of crumbs locked inside his brain, and if he ever got hungry enough for the truth, all he had to do was gather those crumbs. He was in love with a woman who made her bones gathering crumbs.

And he couldn't get away from her fast enough.

Trouble was, he didn't know where to go. Truth was, he was getting hungry. Hungrier by the minute.

It wasn't like he wanted to tell a story or solve a mystery or save anybody but himself. He just wanted to move on. He wanted to take what Logan called the red road—the good way—and he wanted to walk toward a dream, a good dream. He was tired of nightmares, tired of running away.

And so he ended up on his father's doorstep again.

"Did you forget something?"

He'd left Big Boy in Logan's pasture. He'd left the trailer. He'd left all of his training gear. But none of that was forgotten, and his father knew it. Logan could always tell when something needed to be said, even if half the time it never was. But that was Ethan's doing. Logan was always ready to listen.

"Yeah," Ethan said as he took a seat at the kitchen counter. The requisite coffee was being poured. "But I'm afraid it's coming back to me."

"Afraid?" Logan set the steaming cup of black coffee in front of him. *Pejuta sapa.* Brush up on your traditions, Bella kept telling him. He had grown up with Logan's traditions. Maybe more had sunk in than he'd realized.

"I won't be. If I can put it together, I think the fear will go away." He put his hands around the cup, comforted by the heat. "But you might not like it."

"Don't worry about me, Ethan. I have strong shoulders."

"I know. You're a good father. You always were."

He glanced up. "You were a mother, too. You were both."

"I don't know about that. I could say I did my best, but, hell, I could've done better."

Ethan wasn't going to protest. Not now. He had to get the real stuff out before he lost his nerve.

"Did you know my mother was steppin' out on you?"

"I suspected." Logan sipped his coffee. "I should've known, but for a long time I didn't want to."

"Yeah, I know how that goes."

"You were so young," Logan said. "Did you... see something?"

"Yeah, I did. I saw lots of things that didn't seem right." Details. More than he wanted to dwell on. He had to stay on track. "I had to go with her sometimes. Got so I didn't want to, but I didn't want to make a fuss, either. I didn't want to make any trouble." He cleared an unmanly sting from his throat. "I didn't want to lose you."

"You..." Logan was beginning to struggle, too. He didn't want to show it any more than Ethan did. "She'd say she was going to Rapid or Pierre for something, and she was taking you. I didn't like it that she favored you over Trace, but you were younger than he was, so..." Logan drew a deep, unsteady breath. "And I told myself if she had you along, it had to be on the up-and-up, you know?"

Ethan nodded. They were gonna help each other out with this. Try not to look at each other too much. That would be rude.

"Where did she take you?" Logan asked.

"Hotels, sometimes. Parties at big houses. I'd sit in a room and watch TV." Ethan looked up at the ceiling and shook his head. "I couldn't tell you, but, *God,* I wanted you to make it stop."

"I'm sorry."

Ethan nodded. He took a quick drink, let the hot coffee burn his tongue and clear his throat. "I think I saw a man get killed."

"Wh-what?"

It wasn't like Logan to trip over a surprise.

Ethan nodded. "I just came from the Double D. Bella's got this whole political conspiracy theory she's trying to make a story out of,·and, uh…" He gave an openhanded gesture to help pull the words out, keep the report going. "They got to talking about the Tribal leases and your father-in-law, and how he's trying to hang on to land he's been taking for granted because he's got Senator Garth on his side." He glanced at his father. "And you know I don't wanna hear nuthin' about Garth."

Logan nodded.

"Anyway, Hank lets on that his dad used to work for Tutan, and that he got killed. And he starts talking about these hunting parties Tutan used to put on for people like Garth. Political people. Powerful political people."

"What happened to Hank's father?"

"Well, Hank says his body was found on Tutan's property, all decayed and shot up. Tutan said he didn't know anything about it, so…case closed."

Logan grunted in disgust. "One of those federal murder investigations with an Indian corpse. No clues, no witnesses, no arrests."

"There *were* witnesses. And I wasn't the only one." He could feel the heat from Logan's shock, but he couldn't look up as he told him, "Mom was there, too."

He felt the familiar hand take hold of his shoulder. It gave him strength.

"I've been having dreams," he said. "I've had crazy dreams for years. Firecrackers scaring a flock of birds. A man standing up in the tall grass. Blood." He looked into his father's sympathetic eyes. "Lately the dreams have been showing me things I don't remember. But I know they happened. When Hank told us about his dad, I felt like I'd been there."

"Did you tell him?"

"No. It was just a feeling." He shook his head. "No, it's more than that, Dad. It's a fact."

A heavy moment passed.

"What do you want to do?" Logan asked quietly.

"I was just a kid. It was a long time ago. I don't

think anyone'll believe me." Ethan sighed. He felt the pain of that day as keenly as he had twenty years ago.

"Where were you when all this happened?"

"I don't know exactly. She left me in the pickup. I think I got out."

"Damn. You could've been killed."

"She always told me that if I said anything about the parties, you'd send us away. She said we were just having fun." He rested his head in his hand, rubbed his forehead, trying to wipe some of the trouble away. "I was so glad when she left, I just put it out of my mind. All of it."

"I guess we all did."

"I gotta tell somebody." Ethan lifted his head. "Coming from me, it probably won't mean a hill of beans, but..."

"I'll be there."

"It ain't your story."

"But you're my son."

He wanted to tell Hank first. He figured that would be the hardest, even with Logan there to stand by him, but it wasn't. Hank didn't doubt him, and he didn't hold it against him for keeping it to himself all these years. Ethan wondered how the man could take it all in without going off on somebody—or just going off.

"You weren't keeping it a secret," Hank said. "Your mind was protecting you."

"I don't know about that. Had a pretty thick head for a while there. Nothing got through to me. But lately, the last, I don't know, ten years or so, things kept popping up. Something happens to get stuff going in my head at night."

"You've been through a lot in the past ten years," Logan said.

"The thing is, all that stuff makes me look like either a liar or a nutcase. Like I'm just trying to get back at Garth."

"That's for the law to figure out. We know what happened," Logan said.

"Yeah. The law," Ethan echoed.

"That's where the story goes next," Hank said.

"Before that, there's one more person." Ethan gave a dry chuckle. "And she's gonna want to run with the ball. I don't know how we'll prove it, but—"

"We don't have to prove anything," Hank said.

"He's right," Logan said. "We'll turn everything over to the FBI. They have to reopen the case. Get Tutan to talk. Track down everyone who was there."

"What if they find Mom?"

"One more mystery solved." Logan shrugged. "Hell, she deserted us, and we moved on. I divorced her. You grew up. We're on the Red Road." He smiled. "We've found women who know how to love us."

"You for sure. After this bombshell, I'm giving Bella some space."

"Do you want space?"

"I want…" Ethan looked his father in the eye. "I want Bella."

"My advice—and I know you haven't asked, but this is your need-to-know moment—is don't keep it to yourself. Tell her."

"So that's it," Ethan told Bella. She'd met him at Logan's place. He'd said he wanted to show her what they had done with Big Boy, and he did. There was something to be said for bringing the story full circle, bringing it home and showing her that he had done what she'd given him the confidence to do. He'd been truthful with his father. And then he'd been truthful with her. "Pretty far out there, isn't it?"

"It all fits together." She held out her cup to Logan for a refill. Kitchen, frybread, coffee. It was the traditional way. The family way. "You know I'm going to follow this thing as far as I can."

Ethan laughed. "You wouldn't be Warrior Woman if you didn't."

"And you know that if ever I was ahead of you, you just caught up."

No more laughter. Ethan saw the sincerity in her eyes, and he cherished it. He also knew it was true.

"Can I run the camera for you?" he asked. "Carry your water? Saddle your horse?"

"No horse," she said. "You're beautiful on horseback. I just want to watch you."

"Chauffeur you around, then."

"I have to be allowed to do something for *you*," she said sweetly.

"Translation," Ethan said, casting a glance his father's way. "Baby, you ain't gonna drive my car."

Chapter Nine

The man and the horse appeared to be having a little tête-à-tête. Bella could see the man's lips moving as he raked his fingers through the horse's lush mane. Ears standing at attention, the mustang bobbed his head once. After a few more words from the man, the regal buckskin gave his head a quick shake, and the man laughed softly.

She slowed her pace as she approached the corral, thinking this must be the way a woman felt when she happened upon her man patiently sharing a teachable moment with their child. She wanted to turn into a fly and light on the fence post.

But she also wanted to be herself and be welcomed with open arms.

"Are you two planning your strategy for tomorrow?" she asked as she let herself in through the corral gate.

Ethan turned quickly, his eyes betraying his surprise. He glanced down at her feet. "You walkin' on cat's paws, woman?"

Bella grinned as she planted her right heel in the dirt, toe pointed skyard to show off her blindingly white walking tennies. "You like my new sneak-up shoes?"

"New boots, new tennies—you got a thing for shoes?"

"The boots hurt."

"They're not made for walking, honey. That ain't the way to break 'em in." He turned his shoulder to the horse, who then followed him across the corral. "'Course, jumpin' out of my pickup on the fly was a damn good way to break me in. Learned my lesson on takin' *no* for Bella's answer." He rewarded Big Boy with his left hand as he took Bella under his arm on the right.

And she was right where she wanted to be.

"Then it was worth the blisters on my feet."

He glanced down again. "You got blisters?"

"Lessons all around." She slipped her arm around his waist. "Logan just left to pick up his wife at the airport."

"We're alone." He gave her a come-on look.

She glanced up at Big Boy. "How's your strategy coming?"

"So far, so good, now that we've got the place all to ourselves."

"How does that help you win the training competition?"

"Oh, that." He scratched the horse's neck. "We're set, aren't we, Big Boy?"

Big Boy bobbed his head, and they both laughed as the horse snorted and walked away.

"Actually, he's all set. But I need a little encouragement." Ethan turned to her, smiling. The shade from his hat brim fell over her face. "Encourage me."

The back of his neck felt warm under her hand, his hair soft between her fingers. She drew his head down and embraced the surge of female power as she kissed him.

Its effect shone in his eyes. He looked dazed for an instant, but then he took charge and pulled up another alluring smile. "You wanna go inside? Just painted my old bedroom. We could break in the new carpet."

She drew back, answering with a saucy smile of her own. "I don't want to do it in a room full of baby furniture."

"Do what?"

"Give you rug burn."

He chuckled. "No furniture yet. Mary gets to pick that out."

"Still," she said, glancing toward the barn, "I'd be imagining baby furniture. I'd prefer a nice haystack."

He groaned as he took her hand and walked her back to the gate. "Now you've got me thinking baby, nursery, 'Little Boy Blue.' Some encouragement."

"I do my best." She looked up at him. "Hank called me after he met with an FBI field agent at the Rapid City office. They're taking your story seriously."

"You call that your best?"

"They're reopening the case."

"No kidding? Actually digging up the whole thing?" He was genuinely surprised. Skeptical of the kind of reception he might get for his twenty-year-old recollection, he'd gone to the regional FBI office on his own. Sure enough, the agent he'd talked to hadn't seemed too impressed, but he'd taken down all the names Ethan could come up with, along with the dates he'd figured out since he'd put his memory together with Hank's story.

Names, dates and forensics were the facts the agent had said he could check out. A long-buried memory was a little dicey.

What about a long-buried Indian and an unsolved murder? Ethan wanted to know. But he hadn't asked. He wouldn't risk being taken for a smart-ass. Never again. Especially not by a cop.

The agent had said he would be in touch, so Ethan bit his tongue while he offered a handshake. And since that meeting, he sure hadn't been holding his breath. He figured he'd done what he could. But it wasn't until he'd called Bella and then Hank to let them know what he'd done that he felt relieved of a burden he didn't know he'd been carrying.

"I don't know what they'll dig up besides the evidence that's been in storage all these years, but they will search for your mother," Bella said. "And they'll question Dan Tutan and Senator Garth."

"You think it's too late?"

"It's never too late. Murder will out." She gave his hand a quick squeeze. "Eventually."

"Here's one for you." He squeezed back as he opened the gate with his free hand. "'Justice is the constant and perpetual will to allot every man his due.'"

"Oh, I like that." She slid past him and through the gate he held open for her. "Who said it?"

"Some old Roman. I memorized it during my trial. It was on the wall of the courtroom." He closed the gate behind them and turned to her, smiling. "I like it, too. Put it in Warrior Woman's pipe and let her smoke it."

"I hope John Night Horse gets his due. Even if nobody goes to jail, let the truth be told. Let's get it out there."

"That's your job." He glanced past her. Between Bella and the horse standing in the corral behind her he'd found new purpose for his hard-earned freedom.

"My job is to show the truth about Big Boy. Let people see what his kind can do."

"I thought your job was to win the big prize."

"That, too," he said with a wink. Keep it light, he told himself. He didn't want her to think he was counting on the money. It was more about the recognition and how he could use it—along with his education—to neutralize at least one of the strikes he had against him.

Okay, the money would help, too.

He glanced toward their two vehicles, parked side by side. The Square One horse trailer was hitched to his pickup. The boys had painted his name on it, along with a big horseshoe and something that was supposed to be a wolf's paw print but looked more like a high five. Ethan had assured them that it worked either way.

"You wanna hang around and meet my new mom, or should we do the decent thing and get out of their way?"

"I forgot to tell you. They're staying in Rapid City tonight. Logan said to tell you he'll be back in time for the show tomorrow." Bella stepped out ahead of him and turned, smiling, her hand still in his. "And so will I."

"You're not goin' anywhere. I need you with me." With a firm tug he reeled her back and drew her into his arms. "Tonight." He gave her a quick kiss. "Tomorrow."

"If we rule out hay wisps and rug burns, that leaves your father's—"

"We're getting a room."

The hotel at the tribal casino had one vacancy left. The desk clerk told Ethan that this was going be his lucky night and asked what game he would be playing.

"I didn't get lucky 'til I quit gambling," Ethan told the young man. He thought he'd sounded pretty damn clever until Bella mentioned cowboy poker while they were waiting for the elevator. As soon the doors closed he planted a kiss on that smart mouth of hers that left her breathless. He could tell by the way she was looking at him when the doors opened. She didn't seem to notice the guy who gave him a thumbs-up as they stepped off the elevator.

"You won big, huh? Slots or tables?"

"Horses," Ethan quipped.

"Bet on the buckskin," Bella added, all dreamy-eyed.

"Are you nervous about the competition?" she asked gently.

They'd made love twice—once like hungry young lovers who couldn't get enough, once like deliberate, devoted admirers who took it slow and still couldn't quite get enough. They'd lain in each other's arms, stirring now and then to touch and be touched, until she tried to feign sleep in the hope that he could get some rest. It didn't work for either of them. "I'm pumped," he said after a while and pressed a kiss into her hair. "I don't mean to keep you awake."

She gave a soft, pleasured sound. "I'm pretty pumped myself."

"Win or lose, I feel good about Big Boy," he said quietly. "He's in peak condition—nothin' prettier than a lineback buckskin—and he handles like a precision-tuned race car. Better, even. A car's got no heart. Big Boy...size, color, speed, all that's a bonus. Big Boy has heart." He drew a deep breath and blew it out quickly. "Yep. I like our chances."

"You can't lose, Ethan. Even if someone else wins."

"I guess everyone who makes it to the show has the right to feel that way. Sally said a couple of them brought the horses back and dropped out." He chuckled. "And then there's my dad, who pulled his horse from the competition so he wouldn't have to give him up. Gave him to his wife."

"You won't mind giving up Big Boy?"

"Sure, I'll mind. But he's gonna sell high, bring in some serious money for the program."

He took her snuggling against him as his cue to slip his arm beneath her head so she could pillow it on his shoulder. She imagined his thoughts bouncing around wildly in his head, tumbling into the back of his throat and onto his tongue.

"And you can't just walk off with one of these

mustangs without meeting Sally's requirements," he continued. "Actually, the BLM's requirements, but you gotta deal with Sally, and she's got her own smell test."

She smiled to herself, because it was dark and only she knew how deeply she was into him. "Could you pass it?"

"You kiddin'? Not even gonna try. I don't let just any woman get this close to my armpit, you know."

"It's your shoulder I want." An understatement.

"The armpit is like the shoulder's underbelly. Can't have one without the other. But you gotta admit, I clean up pretty good." He gave a deep chuckle. "I'm workin' on it, anyway."

"You don't have to convince me." She turned her head and kissed the closest part of him. Warm skin and hard muscle. "I have a crush on you."

"I'll see your crush and raise you…" He groaned. "Hell, I'm all in, Bella. I'm crazy about you."

"You're raising my crush with your crazy?"

"Yeah." He touched her temple, tucked her hair behind ear and whispered, "I'm crazy in love with you."

She felt light-headed, the rest of her body whooshing out from under her the way it did when she neared the edge of a high place. She didn't even have to look down. She could feel the fall coming.

Stay focused, she told herself. "Is the crazy part the underbelly?"

"Does that scare you?"

"No." She was no liar, but how could she say she wasn't scared? On the other hand, how could she say anything else?

Except maybe that she loved him right back.

"If it ever does, I want you to walk away. I mean that." He kissed the top of her head. "We need time to figure this out. I've never been in love before. Crazy, yes, but love? Uh-uh."

"I don't think I have, either. Unless it's the same as a crush that never went away."

"Maybe that's the underbelly for you, huh? The seed? Maybe we can make it grow."

She had only to lift her head, and he met her halfway for a kiss.

"I like our chances," she whispered.

Mustang Sally's Wild Horse Makeover Horse Show was held at the Sinte rodeo grounds. It was a beautiful, warm autumn day, and the grandstand was packed. Sally Night Horse and her sister, Ann, were in charge of the program. Sally insisted on being called *Master* of Ceremonies—never *mistress*. Ann didn't need a title. She was the detail person. Their husbands were busy moving the show along. When Hank spotted Ethan saddling Big Boy on the shady side of the horse trailer, he took a quick detour, his beautiful yellow Lab, Phoebe, in tow.

"Did you see your brother's horse perform?" Hank asked.

"He looked good, didn't he?"

"Not as good as the rider. Skyler's got a nice seat."

Ethan patted the dog's silky head and grinned. "I'll tell Trace you said so."

"Just don't tell my wife."

Bella stuck her head out the pickup window. "I don't think your wife has anything to worry about."

"No, but I do," Hank said. "Sally has a nice seat, too. Plus a bottomless sleeve full of tricks. Remind me to tell you how we met sometime."

"Can I put that tidbit in my story?" Bella brandished her camera.

"Oh, no. It's not for prime time."

"Sounds like just the kind of anecdote that could help me sell the story."

"Please don't tell Sally that." He glanced up at the crow's nest next to the ring and waved. Sally waved back. "I swear, that woman's ears are better than Phoebe's."

And then the atmosphere changed. Hank shifted, turned slowly and offered Ethan a solemn handshake. "I want to thank you."

Ethan looked down at their clasped hands. "It might not come to anything. You know, legally."

"It's already come to something for us, hasn't it?" Hank laid his hand on Ethan's shoulder. "Some people call it closure. I don't see it that way. The truth opened us up. That's the way I feel."

"So do I."

Hank lifted his chin in Big Boy's direction. "You've got a winner there."

Ethan nodded.

"Hey, Ethan!"

He turned toward the familiar voice. Big Bongo and bigmouth Demsey. Trouble and more trouble, and damned if he wasn't glad to see them. "Who turned you two loose?"

"We're all here," Dempsey said. "Shelly brought us on the bus. She told us not to bother you before the show, but we just wanted to…"

Bongo stuck out a beefy hand. "…wish you luck."

Ethan shook Bongo's hand and ruffled Dempsey's spiky hair. Out of the corner of his eye he noticed that Bella had her camera going again, but he didn't flinch. He was getting used to having her lens pointed his way.

"He needs an oil change," Bongo said.

Ethan laughed. He was up next, and a good laugh was just what he needed.

He was magic. Bella didn't know much about horses, but Big Boy's rider was unrivaled. As long as the judges weren't deducting points for battered cowboy hats, Ethan had first place in the bag.

"I want that horse," the man standing beside her said.

Bella spared him a quick glance. "Trace. I didn't see you there."

"Hard to take your eyes off him, isn't it?"

"Yes, it is." Ethan was putting the horse through a series of reining patterns, seemingly effortlessly.

"We're talking about the buckskin, right?"

Bella had no more glances to spare, but she did smile.

"You think he'd mind if I got in on the bidding?" he asked.

"We're talking about Ethan, right?"

Trace laughed.

"I can't think of anything that would please him more."

After all the riders had shown, the trainers were asked to bring the horses back into the arena and chat up prospective buyers while the judges conferred. Bella covered the activity with her camera. She was charmed by Mark Banyon, the young son of a local teacher named Celia, who had no intention of letting the horse he'd named Flyboy go to just anyone. An interview with the horse's trainer, who introduced himself simply as Cougar, served to reassure her that a disabled veteran's group would be bidding on the horse, and God help anyone who tried to run up the bidding. He and Mark would have easy access to Flyboy, who was destined to become the centerpiece of the therapy program that had enabled Cougar to "rejoin the living" after recovering from his war injuries.

"And if you want a fairytale finale for your story," Cougar told Bella as he reached for Mark's mother's hand, "you can bring your camera to our wedding."

"As long as we get copies of all the pictures," Celia said.

"As long as I can bring a date." Bella nodded toward Ethan, who was chatting up his "new mom" on the other side of the arena.

"That guy?" Cougar smiled and shook his head. "Big showboater, that guy. I don't believe that horse was ever wild. Pretty sure that's a ringer you see there."

Bella returned the smile. "I'm pretty sure Ethan's the best there is."

Cougar laughed. "For a free wedding video I won't argue."

Bella made her way across the arena, pausing here and there for a still shot before sneaking up behind her man of the hour. One thing she'd learned by making the rounds to gather her story was that Big Boy was a big hit, even among Ethan's competitors.

Logan extended his hand. "Bella, come meet my wife."

Ethan turned quickly, smiling when their eyes

met. "I gotta get me some of those sneak-up shoes," he said.

"It's not the shoes," Bella assured him as she took her place in the circle. "It's the Lakota blood. Be prepared to jump out of your skin at least once a week, Mary." She offered Logan's wife a handshake, and then she automatically glanced at her emerging baby bump.

Mary's hand went to her stomach, completing the wordless acknowledgment between women.

Logan clapped a hand on Ethan's shoulder. "You were tired of being the baby, weren't you, son?"

"I'll gladly turn that role over," he agreed. "Is it too late to order up a sister?"

"I've decided to keep us all in suspense," Mary said. "I like the idea of letting the baby surprise us."

"Speaking of surprises…" Logan nodded toward the crow's nest. "Looks like our master of ceremonies has something to tell us."

Sally started out with an order.

"Everyone clear the arena except the trainers and their horses. I'm just as anxious as anybody else, so step lively, folks. I've got some introductions to make, and then we'll get the results from the judges."

Bella looked up at Ethan, smiled, and turned to follow everyone else who'd been excused.

"Oh, wait." Sally's voice boomed. "Everyone except the press."

Bella looked up. Sally nodded. "I don't care whose girlfriend you are, you're still the press."

It took all of about two minutes to empty out the arena. Bella took some footage of the lineup while Zach's brother, Sam, was introduced as the donor of the grand prize. He gave credit to his daughter, Star, who had inherited a winning lottery ticket after her mother's death. Sam didn't mention the source of the money, but Bella knew the story.

Next came the introduction of the judges, who were well-known in the horse world and included an Olympic champion, a man who'd trained horses for the movies, another who trained for the Royal Canadian Mounted Police and a stock show champion. The mustangs had been trained for various styles of riding and different kinds of work or sport. They would prove that mustangs made fine mounts. Their story would bring support for the Double D Wild Horse Sanctuary and for the preservation of the American wild horse.

And the auction would bring much-needed cash to the program. But the auction wouldn't start until the winner was announced, and the microphone was suddenly silent. Those in the arena pretended to ignore the crow's nest. They turned to each other, exchanged a few comments, laughed nervously.

Bella took more video, and then she sidled up to Ethan. He needed some distraction. "Have you met Cougar?" she asked. "The one with that gorgeous Paint."

"You like Paints?" He rubbed his buckskin's cheek. "Don't worry, boy. She's no judge."

"Cougar's an army vet, too. He trained Flyboy to be a service horse. You know, for therapy."

"I saw that. That's some fine work. I could get into that kind of work."

"Yes, you could."

He gave her a tight smile. "I've got a ways to go, though, haven't I?"

"Time or distance?" She slipped her hand into his and gave a quick squeeze. "Either way, I'm right beside you."

Ethan turned to her, and for a moment everything around them receded. He didn't care where he was or what else was going on. Wherever, whatever, Bella was with him. All was right with the world, and he told her so with a wink and a smile.

There was movement in the crow's nest. The Night Horses appeared first. Then the Zach Beaudrys. Then the Sam Beaudrys. And finally the judges.

"Here comes the announcement," Bella said.

"And the twenty-thousand dollar award for the best mustang trainer in the first annual Mustang Sally's Wild Horse Makeover Horse Show goes to…"

Ethan kept his cool when his name was called, but Bella did not. Her kiss would have shocked her public. The details of her whispered promise of a private celebration set his ear aflame. His sober, sensible, traditional Bella nearly knocked him off his feet.

For the second time.

And he was damn sure it wouldn't be the last.

* * * * *

REQUEST YOUR FREE BOOKS!

2 FREE NOVELS PLUS 2 FREE GIFTS!

 Harlequin

SPECIAL EDITION

Life, Love & Family

YES! Please send me 2 FREE Harlequin® Special Edition novels and my 2 FREE gifts (gifts are worth about $10). After receiving them, if I don't wish to receive any more books, I can return the shipping statement marked "cancel." If I don't cancel, I will receive 6 brand-new novels every month and be billed just $4.49 per book in the U.S. or $5.24 per book in Canada. That's a saving of at least 14% off the cover price! It's quite a bargain! Shipping and handling is just 50¢ per book in the U.S. and 75¢ per book in Canada.* I understand that accepting the 2 free books and gifts places me under no obligation to buy anything. I can always return a shipment and cancel at any time. Even if I never buy another book, the two free books and gifts are mine to keep forever.

235/335 HDN FEGF

Name	(PLEASE PRINT)	
Address		Apt. #
City	State/Prov.	Zip/Postal Code

Signature (if under 18, a parent or guardian must sign)

Mail to the **Reader Service:**
IN U.S.A.: P.O. Box 1867, Buffalo, NY 14240-1867
IN CANADA: P.O. Box 609, Fort Erie, Ontario L2A 5X3

Not valid for current subscribers to Harlequin Special Edition books.

Want to try two free books from another line?
Call 1-800-873-8635 or visit www.ReaderService.com.

* Terms and prices subject to change without notice. Prices do not include applicable taxes. Sales tax applicable in N.Y. Canadian residents will be charged applicable taxes. Offer not valid in Quebec. This offer is limited to one order per household. All orders subject to credit approval. Credit or debit balances in a customer's account(s) may be offset by any other outstanding balance owed by or to the customer. Please allow 4 to 6 weeks for delivery. Offer available while quantities last.

Your Privacy—The Reader Service is committed to protecting your privacy. Our Privacy Policy is available online at www.ReaderService.com or upon request from the Reader Service.

We make a portion of our mailing list available to reputable third parties that offer products we believe may interest you. If you prefer that we not exchange your name with third parties, or if you wish to clarify or modify your communication preferences, please visit us at www.ReaderService.com/consumerschoice or write to us at Reader Service Preference Service, P.O. Box 9062, Buffalo, NY 14269. Include your complete name and address.

Sometimes love strikes in the most unexpected circumstances...

Soon-to-be single mom Antonia Wright isn't looking for romance, especially from a cowboy. But when rancher and single father Clayton Traub rents a room at Antonia's boardinghouse, Wright's Way, she isn't prepared for the attraction that instantly sizzles between them or the pain she sees in his big brown eyes. Can Clay and Antonia trust their hearts and build the family they've always dreamed of?

Don't miss

THE MAVERICK'S READY-MADE FAMILY

by Brenda Harlen

Montana
★ MAVERICKS
BACK IN THE SADDLE

Available this October from Harlequin® Special Edition®

*What happens when a Texas nanny learns she is
the biological daughter of a prince? Her rancher boss
steps in to help protect her from the paparazzi, but who
can protect her from her attraction to him?*

Read on for an excerpt of
A HOME FOR NOBODY'S PRINCESS
by USA TODAY *bestselling author Leanne Banks.*

Available October 2012

"This is out of control." Benjamin sighed. "Well, damn. I guess I'm gonna have to be your fiancé."

Coco's jaw dropped. "What?"

"It won't be real," he said quickly, as much for himself as for her. After the debacle of his relationship with Brooke, the idea of an engagement nearly gave him hives. "It's just for the sake of appearances until the insanity dies down. This way it won't look like you're all alone and ready to have someone take advantage of you. If someone approaches you, then they'll have to deal with me, too."

She frowned. "I'm stronger than I seem," she said.

"I know you're strong. After what you went through for your mom and helping Emma to settle down, I know you're strong. But it's gotta be damn tiring to feel like you've always got to be on guard."

Coco sighed and her shoulders slumped. "You're right about that." She met his gaze with a wince. "Are you sure you don't mind doing this?"

"It's just for a little while," he said. "You mentioned that a fiancé would fix things a few minutes ago. I had to run it through my brain. It seems like the right thing to do."

She gave a slow nod and bit her lip. "Hmm. But it would cut into your dating time."

Benjamin laughed. "That's not a big focus at the moment."

"It would be a huge relief for me," she admitted. "If you're sure you don't mind. And we'll break it off the second you feel inconvenienced."

"No problem," he said. "I'll spread the word. Should be all over the county by lunchtime. No one can know the truth. That's the only way this will work."

Coco took a deep breath and closed her eyes as if preparing to take a jump into deep water. "Okay" she said, and opened her eyes. "Let's do it."

Will Coco be able to carry out the charade?

Find out in Leanne Banks's new novel—
A HOME FOR NOBODY'S PRINCESS.

Available October 2012 from Harlequin® Special Edition®

HARLEQUIN Romance

At their grandmother's request, three estranged
sisters return home for Christmas to the small town
of Beckett's Run. Little do they know that this family
reunion will reveal long-buried secrets…
and new-found love.

Discover the magic of Christmas in a brand-new
Harlequin® Romance miniseries.

In October 2012, find yourself
SNOWBOUND IN THE EARL'S CASTLE
by **Fiona Harper**

Be enchanted in November 2012 by a
SLEIGH RIDE WITH THE RANCHER
by **Donna Alward**

And be mesmerized in December 2012 by
MISTLETOE KISSES WITH THE BILLIONAIRE
by **Shirley Jump**

Available wherever books are sold.

celebrating 15 YEARS

Love Inspired™

Another heartwarming installment of

—◄ **TEXAS TWINS** ►—

**Two sets of twins, torn apart by family secrets,
find their way home**

When big-city cop Grayson Wallace visits an elementary
school for career day, he finds his heartstrings
unexpectedly tugged by a six-year-old fatherless boy and
his widowed mother, Elise Lopez. Now he can't get the
struggling Lopezes off his mind. All he can think about
is what family means—especially after discovering
the identical twin brother he hadn't known he had
in Grasslands. Maybe a trip to ranch country is just
what he, Elise and little Cory need.

Look-Alike Lawman
by Glynna Kaye

*Available October 2012
wherever books are sold.*

www.LoveInspiredBooks.com

LI87770